'Howard G. Awbery has a laid-back style of writing, crafting romance and intrigue. He seduces his readers who suddenly find themselves on the edge of their seats… and it's long past midnight!'

A Sprig of Mint

'A Sprig of Mint' is dedicated to my long suffering family, all my patient friends, the amazingly generous Llandrillo villagers and anyone else who, like me, has been intoxicated by the mystical atmosphere of a stone circle.

Illustrated by James Bucklow

www.fast-print.net/store.php

A SPRIG OF MINT
Copyright © Howard G Awbery 2013

A catalogue record for this book is available from the British Library

ISBN 978-178035-741-6

First published 2013 by FASTPRINT PUBLISHING
of Peterborough, England.

A Sprig of Mint

1

James sank down in front of the biggest stone in the circle to regain his breath. The walk to the stone circle had been anything but 'a gentle walk for the active elderly' as the guidebook described. Fit as he was at thirty, the last 400 yards uphill had stretched him. He unzipped his 'breathable' jacket and allowed the steam to escape from his perspiration-wet shirt. What little breeze there was felt decidedly cold on his newly exposed chest and neck. James stretched and allowed his aching muscles to relax, slid his rucksack off one shoulder first and then the other and allowed it drop to the floor. This was his exact routine when he arrived at home he mused; arriving at this stone circle felt like just like coming home to him. Even Meg, his sleek, black and white border collie wove her way in and out of the circle of familiar stones like a circus dog smelling every inch.

For James the geography of stone circles intrigued him, the history of stone circles fascinated him and the mystery of stone circles bewitched him. Inspired to explore their very meaning, he had visited some twenty stone circles since he was first introduced to the concept and his imagination for their origins was re-ignited every time he stepped inside one. Why were they here, what was their purpose, who built them and were there patterns in their positions across the country. How had they survived for between three and five thousand years?

This site, called Moel Ty Uchaf, was perched high on the Berwyn Mountains in North Wales and had become a favourite for James for two reasons. First, Moel Ty Uchaf was such an amazing place of solitude and tranquillity that bathed away the stresses of his cutthroat, corporate existence. James dealt in financial transactions taking place across continents, across twenty-four hours, non-stop. Not real money, but electronic money moving in and out of off-shore accounts, into and out of ghost corporations and then back to the UK for 9.00 a.m. when the whole round started again; all within international law. He regretted he never held anything in his hands at the end of the week; there was nothing tangible for him to touch after all his efforts, only numbers on endless balance sheets. Whenever he was to leave this earth there would be nothing to put his hand upon and claim, 'I, James did that', whereas, the stone circles were real. The stone circles were different; built by the sweat of many who believed unquestionably in the legacy of the stones, their value and, of course, their hidden secrets. Their longevity and mystery had taxed the brains of the best historians and archaeologists across the world for centuries.

The second reason Moel Ty Uchaf was James's favourite stone circle was the nearest village called Llandrillo. A delightful muddle of a village consisting of whitewashed and stone built houses spread higgledy-piggledy from the junction of two valleys and two rivers. In its history, Llandrillo had been a centre for horse-trading and at that time boasted fourteen pubs and the trade to support them; now it had but one pub. The ancients of the village talked of the strings of horses, Fell ponies and Shires that trotted and cantered proudly along the cobbled streets of Llandrillo in years gone by. They talked affectionately of magnificent greys, pretty palominos, noble bays and proud stallions as if it were yesterday, now all gone.

Now Llandrillo was a quiet village of gentle folk renowned for their generosity and kindness to others who were less well off than themselves. Thousands and thousands of pounds were collected annually for hospices, major charities and individual good causes.

Amazingly, the Royal Commission on Ancient and Historical Monuments of Wales decreed, in its wisdom, that the cheerful red telephone box in the centre of Llandrillo, with its domed roof and four lunettes from the reign of George VI, should become a listed building; a decision that would have had the designer, Sir Giles Gilbert Scott laughing out loud with a mixture of pride and incredulity that there was nothing else in this ancient village of a more worthy note.

Llandrillo had transformed itself a dozen times over the last three thousand years eventually settling five miles from Corwen to the west, seven miles from Bala in the east and only two miles up the Old Drover's Road from the stone circle of Moel Ty Uchaf.

But what was so special for James was the fact that the village of Llandrillo boasted a Georgian, Michelin star 'Restaurant with Rooms' called Tyddyn Llan; here in abject comfort he made his base camp. James started every day with a superb, full, Welsh breakfast and ended every day being wowed by the choice and quality of food. As a regular he was always made to feel welcome; nothing was too much trouble and the service was exemplary.

Tyddyn Llan's lounge was a delightful furniture melee of Regency, Chinese and Georgian mixed with the comfort of modern. Guests were transported through the ages allowing them to choose the level of comfort depending on their mood. An inordinate number of sculptured ducks pervaded the lounge and the walls were hung with the efforts of the artists' weekend retreats. Two brass miner's flame lamps adorned the stone mantle piece linking this sleepy agricultural setting in North Wales with Wales's industrial past. The story goes that the two flame lamps belonged to the owner's family. One flame lamp belonged to a deputy in the pit and the other to a member of coal mining industry's most revered of professions; that of the Mines Rescue Brigade. The Mines Rescue Brigade members were the heroes of the underground world and were first on the scene following some of the worst coal mining disasters ever recorded.

Hotel guests' outfits for dinner at Tyddyn Llan ranged from the wholly inappropriate and unaware sporting Pringle sweaters, to the respectful, compliant, jacketed owners of the modern day 'grey pound'. Complete with Cavalry Twill trousers and Brogues, the modern day owners of the 'grey pound' defiantly departed from convention by making a token statement of being in the twenty first century by deliberately omitting to wear a tie. Ladies moved between twin suits and elegant, flowing silk outfits. Tyddyn Llan was populated by retirees, D.I.N.K.Ys, the hunting, shooting, fishing brigade, intrepid walkers, dusty historians and oblivious lovers. The oblivious lovers were easily spotted linked together continuously by touch, celebrating private anniversaries, stolen weekends or both, comfortably lost under their 'Harry Potter cloaks' in a village far beyond the reaches of the most high-tech Satellite Navigation system's capability.

James always booked Room 1, a room tastefully merging antiques, style and function. An antique, four-poster bed complete with Egyptian cotton graced the bedroom and a high backed bath welcomed him after yomping across the Berwyn Mountains. A choice of his favourite single malts was always within easy reach of the bath.

The romance of this splendid room was lost on James, for he always came alone, but Tyddyn Llan's opulence, homeliness, quality and craftsmanship of the furniture was not. However, for this visit his plans had been completely upset at the last minute due to a financial crisis in the Boardroom. The finance meeting had run on and on the previous night, in fact it was so late when it finished that his only option was to make a very early start for Moel Ty Uchaf from

London the next day. That in turn, had prevented James from having his leisurely, full Welsh breakfast at Tyddyn Llan.

At this precise moment, facing the centre of the stone circle and sitting with his back against the biggest stone, his stomach took precedence over his fascination with stone circles. The financial crisis he had faced the previous night floated away with the wispy clouds and despite the magnificent surroundings, right now, his stomach felt like his throat had been cut. James rummaged into the depths of his well-travelled rucksack and brought out a bundle covered in tin foil like a rabbit out of a hat. Next came his trusty flask of tomato soup, always tomato soup. An apple to finish and he had a feast fit for a fell walker. James set his lunch out on the grass in front of him. He unwrapped the outer tinfoil and took out two sandwiches, one of cheese and one of meat, each the size of doorsteps. Selecting the cheese sandwich in one hand he eased himself to his feet and turned to look at the view.

The view was amazing wherever he looked. He walked slowly from stone to stone, stopping to look out at a slightly different view from every stone. He munched as he viewed the distant horizons. Whoever had originally built this circle must have looked out on the same horizons and marvelled at the same rugged beauty James was looking at right now. Whoever had selected this spot for this monument had chosen one of the most beautiful places in Wales. What strength of character to believe it could be done, what determination to build it in such a remote location and what vision that it would remain untouched for at least three thousand years.

His view was assisted by the day, a clear-blue, warm, mid-summer day with just the occasional cloud. In the distance, all around him were the flat mountain tops, aged and smoothed by rain and wind over millennia. James felt as if he could reach out and stroke their rolling contours.

The range was generously called the Berwyn Mountains, not real mountains, not like the Alps or even Snowdon. These mountains were high, flat expanses joined by ridges and saddles, their tops dotted with Cairns to mark the paths, beautiful in their own rugged right. The mountains resembled the folds and curves of Mother Nature's green duvet, the contours following her slumbering body beneath. The Berwyn Mountains displayed a distinctive welcoming character for summer walkers and those who enjoyed stark, natural beauty - but the mountains were not playgrounds in the winter. The fierce winds raced unimpeded across the flat mountaintops dropping the temperature to 20 degrees below. The stone circle had been built proudly to withstand the summer droughts and the winter rains and winds.

Green cultivated valley fields and lowland grazing areas were delineated by arrow straight stonewalls, monuments built with the foresight of farming folk in recent history to be maintenance free for generations to come. The stone walls became smaller as they disappeared into the distance, enclosing fields sprinkled with sheep; small, tough, Welsh, hill-sheep. Sheep continually being washed pure white by the Welsh wetting rain and then dried, combed and fluffed up like white pillows by the horizontal winds that stroked the fields and bent the long grass flat. Sheep unconcernedly continuing their life of chewing the rich grass and waiting to be rinsed and blown dry time and time again.

As the slopes of the mountains became steeper, James noticed that fences replaced the walls; the fences eventually giving way to a mantle sweeping over the mountain tops of robust, weathered heather. He saw the colours change from lush green in the valley up through lighter greens and browns of the rougher grazing and long grass, to the mottled purple and mauves of the flowers of the heather. James moved around the 41 stones in the circle marvelling at the beauty as he looked out at 41 different views. He had just finished munching on the cheese doorstep when he arrived back at the first stone.

Today was his birthday and knowing he was coming up here on his own when he shopped yesterday, he had treated himself to his favourite sandwich fillings. His wife, who had no interest in stone circles or the great outdoors or in fact James, rarely packed a lunch for him and if she did it was a pair of uninspiring, grated cheese and lettuce leaf sandwiches made with cotton wool bread he could see through. How he hated grated cheese. So, when he discovered she was going away for a long weekend with her 'friends' James had shopped with a vengeance.

Fearing that the financial meeting would delay his departure the previous night he had bought a tidy nog of Caerphilly cheese from Mayfair's cheese shop, just down from his office. At 5.00am this morning he had sliced it down the middle. A 3/8in thick slice of raw, mauve onion came next and incomplete without a table spoon of luminous yellow Piccalilli, he arranged the whole gastronomic volcano of taste inside two thick, wholesome slices of 'bad as it gets' white bread. The second sandwich was a 1/8 inch thick slice of ox-tongue painted generously in English mustard topped by a slice of a beef tomato again in an eiderdown of heavy-duty white bread. Half the fun of the excursion was the preparation of his lunch. James reflected on the fact he had become excited by the planning and preparation of his lunch!

Right now, just before mid-day, he decided his wife and her friends would still be shopping. Swinging oversized designer label bags housing outrageously costly little dresses for functions to which they had not yet been invited... just in case. They would then head for a wine bar for Rose spritzers and exorbitantly expensive salads. His wife had gymed down to a size 8, ate leaves, appetite inhibitors, celery and drank copious amounts of cranberry juice. To be fair to her, James had to admit she did have an amazing figure and she was determined to stay shapely. Children played no part in her plans; the risk to her figure was too great, whereas James went to the gym spasmodically but was blessed with a metabolism that burnt everything he ate and drank without putting on an ounce. She hated him for it.

His wife saw her friends as competitors in the personal weight reduction race, a race in which she had no desire of coming second. When he did listen in to her and her friends' conversations it usually had something to do with tummy tucks, anti-aging creams, colonic irrigation or figure enhancing surgery. James and his wife had grown apart and both knew it. He had wanted to come home to a wife and children and just chat over dinner, someone with whom he could share the day's little triumphs. They rarely ate together and their interests had diverged early in their relationship. She on the other hand had needed the appearance of a stable relationship for her CV.

The physical closeness between them had slowly diluted to a brother/sister relationship. It was marginally more convenient to stay together than to split up. It suited them both, just at this moment. They both had good jobs and wanted for nothing material. He was not demanding of her, she on the other hand had tired of him but tolerated him. He was able to follow his interest despite her occasional scorn and she hers, whatever that was. They both knew that if ever a storm broke between them it would be over. Things would be said that would make a return to their 'comfortable, convenient' arrangement albeit impossible. This unnatural calm was the best option. They both knew it.

James tried to combine his desire to stay reasonably fit by walking to stone circles across the UK with his thirst for an understanding of the Late Bronze Age. That blurred period in history around 1000 years BC when copper from the Great Orme's Head in North Wales was mixed with tin from other parts of the country like Cornwall, to make the considerably harder material, bronze. The finds of small, double-bladed axes called pelstaves made from bronze were a credit to the smiths of the era, their talents being applied not only to war but also to working the land. James was intrigued by the recent research conducted on ancient civilisations like the understanding of the value of crop rotation and manuring the land to retain soil fertility; simple but sound agricultural practices being carried out 3000 years ago. He was intrigued by the start of the stratification of societies, with the introduction of tools, weapons and jewellery. He was intrigued by the concept of societies joining forces for strength, for security, for larger herds, less inbreeding and ultimately more wealth. But his particular fascination was in the differing ways they buried their dead. Stone circles, tumuli and cremation sites were just some of the burial practices of the time.

Despite his high-powered City job, he never wanted to lose being grounded by a real interest. Circles had become his passion and Moel Ty Uchaf his favourite. Here he could relax, here he could think, here he felt a connection, here he felt strangely at home.

James let his mind drift across the range of opportunities over the recent years he had allowed to pass him by. Had he stayed in the army he would now have been made up to major with all the physical excitement and mental stimulation he could ever want. He sometimes yearned for the camaraderie of his men. Camaraderie earned in the face of fierce fighting on unauthorised mission after unauthorised mission. He missed the black humour and banter of his men. He missed their closeness and the feeling of them always covering his back whether in one war or another, in civvies or combat. However, there were just so many escapades he could expect to scrape out from, just so many times he could recover from the loss of men under his command. James felt he had dispatched himself with alacrity and left the army just one mission before his last.

The alternative to full combat duties or leaving the army completely was an army desk job in London as an ambassador for the service, a role where he would have to thread his way between short-termism and political myopia. James wasn't sure he could take on a role fighting arrogant, safe politicians on behalf of his men in the front line, the men who he had left behind to fight. James concluded it was a role to which he believed there would be no wins, only frustration and disappointment with his own performance. He believed his insignificant impact would result in a feeling of failure after failure against the established system. He decided he couldn't live with himself with that level of continuous failure, for he was too close to the reality of war and the shortages of equipment; it would have become too personal for him.

Therefore, on demob, he had accepted an opportunity to join a financial boutique in the City. He had been headhunted and, as such, been flattered and financially seduced. Quickly, he replaced real, personal, physical danger with career dangers. He orientated a new type of stimulation by commercial, cerebral combat and enemy action in the Boardroom.

He had found his place in life for this moment in time and, as such, considered himself to be contented.

After looking out over the Berwyn Mountains from every stone James sat back again against the largest stone looking in towards the centre of the circle.

Meg knew the routine and lay down alongside him in her normal pose, one paw over his out-stretched legs so, even if she slept, which she hardly ever did, her master couldn't move without her knowing. Satisfied with lunch, he closed his eyes and clasped his hands behind his head. James leaned back, turned his face up to the sky letting the mid-summer's day sunshine wash over him. It didn't get any better than this he told himself. As the 'doorstep' and soup slipped down inside him so did his level of consciousness. A sleep after lunch was his routine after a 5.00 am start, a 200-mile drive and a rigorous walk in the fresh air. He felt safe in the knowledge that he was being watched over by his canine guard.

2

James was sleeping in an uncomfortable position and try as he might to rearrange himself without waking up fully he didn't seem able. Something was digging into his back. Eventually, he leaned forward in his hazy half-asleep state and reached back with one hand to feel what was causing him so much discomfort.

It was a wedge of some description. A wedge, fixed to a huge stone in a stone circle? It wasn't there when he had fallen asleep. It didn't make any sense.

James opened his eyes and rubbed his sore back. Looking around he became aware that things were not exactly as they had been when he went to sleep only a few moments ago. Meg stood up, shook herself and looked about curiously. James turned to get up only to find that he was no longer leaning against the biggest stone in the stone circle, but against the solid wooden wheel of an old cart. What had woken him was the wooden wedge that kept the wheel in place on the cart's wooden axle. This didn't make any sense at all.

James stood up abruptly, not all the stones were in place that were there before he fell asleep. On the back of the cart he recognised the very stone he had been leaning against earlier. A big white horse on the other end of the cart snorted as it chomped contentedly in its nosebag. There had been no horse or cart before he had gone to sleep. James turned around and around trying to focus on something familiar that had been there when he had gone to sleep. There was nothing. James clutched his rucksack to himself and stroked Meg reassuringly as they both tried to make some order of the new scene. Meg was staying close to his leg looking very uncomfortable, her ears up high and the rest of her senses on high alert. James rubbed his eyes. What on earth was happening? Where was he? What had happened to the rest of the circle? What the hell was going on?

Walking around the stones James counted only 20 out of the original 41 and they were much higher than he remembered. He noted the positions of the absent stones had been marked out roughly on the ground. He looked at the horse and cart. The construction of the cart was heavy timber covered in scuffmarks from years of work. The wheels were solid wood, splintered and chipped by miles of travel over rough tracks and the horse's reins and harness were crude but practicable. The big white horse, despite its age, was in good shape. Its mane, tail and forelock had been brushed and its stomach was full. The horse was obviously well cared for and its blinkered head continued to munch contentedly in the strong rope bag.

James tried to clear his head; a mixture of anxiety and incredulity overcame him. Meg was so close to him he could feel her against his leg all the time for reassurance as she looked furtively around.

In the distance the heather that, just a few moments ago, had only covered the top of the mountains, now covered all the mountains and flowed like mauve icing running down the sides of a cake right down into the valley to jigsaw into the forests. Now there were no fences, there were no walls, just trees. There were forests of trees. There were trees in the valleys, there were trees as far as he could see, they were everywhere. Trees planted randomly by Mother Nature creating their own unique patterns of size and colour. Not rows upon rows of accurately planted, characterless, dark, cash-generating, foreign pines, but mixtures and swathes of different indigenous, deciduous trees all in full leaf. James leaned against a stone and tried to make sense of it all. He looked at the time 12.10pm he had only been asleep ten minutes, how could all this have happened in ten minutes?

It was then that James felt he wasn't alone. Someone, somewhere was close. He felt uncomfortable, that army night patrol behind enemy lines uncomfortable, and he didn't know why. However, under the circumstances, it wasn't surprising. Meg growled a long, low, deep growl that said to James that someone was close by. "Bandits?" asked James of Meg, and with that Meg lay down as if she was herding sheep, her nose on her paws pointing in the direction of the 'bandit'. Bandits to them had always meant anybody in the vicinity invading their private space.

Huffing and puffing up the slope struggled a man in what looked like a monk's off-white, flowing habit. He was sixtyish, about 5ft 3ins tall, slim build, wearing a brown, weather-beaten complexion. The 'monk' approached the circle. He called to James when he was still a little way off.

"You must be from yon village?" he puffed as he walked towards James, "I prayed to the gods for some help with this particularly big stone, forgive me mentioning it but you do wear some strange garb, what name does your dog go by?" all this tumbled out in one gasping sentence.

James stood still watching and listening to this oddly dressed character and his unfamiliar dialect. He didn't seem to be a threat.

"May the gods preserve me; they've sent me a mute!" declared the 'monk' looking up at the sky in frustration holding his hands out in supplication. Then there followed a change in the 'monk's' tone.

"I need to change the way I'm thinking," admonished the 'monk' of himself.

"I need to thank the gods for any small mercies," and then up really close to James's face the 'monk' shouted, "CAN YOU HEAR ME?"

James stared warily at the 'monk', then he turned and looked at the recently appeared horse and cart, and then he surveyed the incomplete stone circle and looked back at the 'monk' and asked, "Who the hell are you? And where the hell are we?"

"May the gods preserve us all? He's not a mute and he blasphemes as well as me. We'll get on famously," replied the 'monk' laughing out loud and slapping James's shoulder affectionately.

The 'monk' continued, "I, my dear fellow, am a priest. I am called Barnaby of the Llangollen settlement. I am a dreamer. My purpose in life is to dream, and when dreams have been dreamt, I fulfil those dreams, it has been my destiny to dream on behalf of the gods."

James looked blankly at him and shook his head from side to side. Of all the people, thought James, to bump into on the top of a mountain when the world is not as you left it, just a little while since, is a crazy character wearing a smock!

"Look, my dear fellow," said the 'monk' affectionately putting his hand on James's shoulder, "you look confused. My experience is that confusion always comes with a lack of food so how about we share what vitals you have in your sack and then try to unravel the mysteries of the universe on full stomachs? What say you?"

James obediently passed Barnaby his second sandwich and watched him carefully unravel the strange silver paper. Once inside, he sniffed the tongue, mustard and tomato sandwich and looked at James to confirm it wasn't poison. The priest's growling stomach won the battle over caution and he was soon half way through the sandwich before he realised he'd not offered any to James. He limply offered the remains to James who shook his head to Barnaby's great delight. James had no appetite now. Barnaby slowed his eating pace and savoured each mouthful.

With bits spitting out of the corners of his mouth he eyed James up and down and asked, "And what did you say your name was young fellow?"

James told him and also told him he had come to visit the stone circle.

"How in the names of all the god's did you know it was here? Nobody but that old horse and me know it's here," queried Barnaby.

James continued a little louder this time, his frustration evident. All the while he was speaking he was looking around, looking for someone else, anyone else to talk to.

"Right, I'll tell you again," repeated James, "when I first came to this circle, it was all here, all 41 stones of it. Then I went to sleep. When I woke up, half of it had disappeared; a horse and cart had arrived and then up popped a monk."

"I told you before, I'm not, as you call me, a monk, I'm a priest and I've not built the circle yet, so how can you have seen it all?" asked the confused Barnaby. James shook his head and sat on one of the larger stone. Meg in the meantime was eyeing the 'monk' suspiciously but curiosity got the better of her, she edged closer and closer to him. Eventually, Meg nestled against the 'monk's leg which was enough for James to feel slightly more comfortable about him.

The 'monk' reached down and stroked her ears. Meg closed her eyes in contentment. Meg had never been wrong yet about folks' characters. Meg hated all James's wife's friends.

James turned again to Barnaby and asked, "Who are you again and what did you say your name was? In fact what year is it?" From his extensive reading about stone circles he believed the circles had been built as burial sites about three to five thousand years ago, "So I must be in the late Bronze age," he absently said to himself.

"My name is Barnaby... I am a priest... As I said, I come from the Llangollen settlement... I don't know what year it is and neither do I care. I don't know what the Bron... Bron... Bronze age is and again, neither do I care," said Barnaby very slowly so as not to alienate his new worker."

"What I do care about is this stone circle and its construction."

They stood looking at each other wondering who was the maddest for a good few minutes when the jovial Barnaby broke the uncomfortable silence by handing James a heavy, long handed shovel and said, "If you have such an interest in stone circles young fellow then perhaps you can help me finish this one?"

James absently took the shovel and after a few moments contemplating the bizarre situation started to dig where the priest pointed with his sandaled foot.

"Oh, what the Hell? How deep?" asked James with a resigned sigh.

"About a quarter of the length of the stone needs to be in the ground for it to be secure with the winds and rains up here," replied Barnaby.

James started to dig with the clumsy, rude wooden spade and a pick made from the antlers of a deer.

Twice while he was digging he stopped abruptly and said out loud to himself, "This is crazy," threw the clumsy spade down and went across to try to make some sense out of the priest. Each time the priest patiently answered all of his questions as well as he could for someone who was living in a time, three thousand years earlier.

"Where did you say was the nearest village?"

"Along yonder path."

"What's it called?"

"Llandrillo."

"How many people live there?"

"Many."

"Why are you building the circle?"

"For the gods."

"What do you mean 'for the gods'?"

"Do you need me, an old priest to help you, a young man to finish digging the hole?"

The challenge was enough to re-motivate James. Two hours later, down to a T-shirt, sweating profusely and with blistered hands, James called to Barnaby who was marking out the next holes with an unexpected accuracy.

Barnaby checked the hole, congratulated James on its depth, and together they encouraged the horse to reverse the cart with great precision towards the hole. Barnaby spragged both wheels and commenced rubbing pig fat onto the exposed leather skin that was half under the stone. He then carefully started to ratchet the end of the cart nearest the horse upwards. When the cart reached its tipping point the huge stone moved slowly on the slippery leather surface and, in a very controlled manner, slid perfectly into the hole. This was not the first time Barnaby and the horse had worked together and it showed, thought James. Each knew what the other required and when Barnaby whispered something into the horse's ear, it whinnied, moved away about five paces and then stopped.

They made some slight adjustments to the stone with long wooden levers and then stood back to admire their work. The stone would stand majestically in its place for who knows how long? James could confirm at least the first three thousand years.

James congratulated Barnaby on his handiwork. He was enjoying a strange sense of satisfaction but not understanding whether it was for the simple act of exhausting physical work of digging the hole and positioning the stone, or the fact that he was part of something that would confuse and tax the brains of historians for ever. James turned to Barnaby and put his hand in the air to do a 'high five' forgetting he was in a strange time three thousand years earlier.

"What happens now?" asked James as he loaded the tools onto the cart.

Leading the horse away from the circle Barnaby shouted back to him, "Now we go and find another stone, dig it up, bring it up here and plant it alongside that one and watch the circle grow," and with that Barnaby laughed out loud to the world.

With no one else to talk to, nowhere else to go and no way of returning, James decided to engage fully with this strange character and he and Meg dutifully followed.

Barnaby led them down the familiar Old Drover's Road to the village of Llandrillo. It had changed beyond recognition from the Llandrillo James had passed through earlier that morning. Now it consisted of about 35, round, thatched dwellings nestled in the valley by the river. The main road had disappeared and a muddy rutted track was in its place, now the church had gone and stock pens stood in its place, now the bridge was gone and they splashed through the shallow river. There was nothing that James vaguely recognised.

As he entered the village James was amazed how accurate the pictures he'd seen in books about late Bronze Age settlements had been. Wicker pens for keeping pigs stood all around them, frames stretching skins to dry in the sun in rows faced the sun and bundles of reeds for thatching were stacked up high near the skeleton of a partly formed round house. Men were dressed in heavy shirts devoid of colour and the women were dressed in shapeless shift style dresses dyed randomly by berry juice or cochineal, the colours faded unevenly by the sun. Both men and women eyed him suspiciously and stood in groups watching James and Barnaby approach, their only comfort being the fact that James was accompanied by Barnaby, otherwise his welcome might not have been this cordial.

Despite the warm August day cooking fires smoked outside some of the houses. Barnaby and James were quickly surrounded by a flock of excited children who fought to hold their hands and excitedly tugged at James's strange cagoule and rucksack. He regretted not having any sweets for the children but Meg was having a whale of a time with all the attention and stick throwing. Every villager acknowledged Barnaby as he passed their homes, obviously a priest of some standing; nobody made eye contact with James. Together they led the old horse to a lean-to stable a little distance from the other houses. There they unhitched the heavy cart and brushed the weary horse down. They removed the harness and then proceeded to carefully remove the burrs that clung to the horse's fetlocks. With fresh water and a manger full of oats, the big horse settled for the night.

Barnaby's rustic house was the biggest thatched dwelling on the outskirts of the village. Inside it felt surprisingly cool to James despite a smouldering fire at one end. The floor was covered in reeds and around the sides of the building shelves were stacked with herbs and bunches of drying leaves alongside jugs and pots. Just like his garage at home James believed Barnaby knew where everything was despite the jumbled appearance. At one end of the room a bed of sticks and straw was topped with a crumpled blanket. Beneath the rough-hewn beams, yellowing tallow candles hung, each haloed by a black smoke ring on the reed roof. Over the embers of the fire a cooking pot dangled from a wooden trivet and the smell of the broth made James's stomach rumble in the memory of just half of his lunch.

Barnaby cleared some pots and half chopped herbs from the uneven table and gestured for James to sit down opposite on the end of an equally uneven bench. He proceeded to set out two wooden bowls, two wooden spoons and two leather beakers. Barnaby humped the heavy iron pot over to the table and ladled two generous portions of the gloopy contents into the bowls. Then he humped the heavy iron pot back to the fire and gave it a stir with a nearby stick, finally giving the fire an automatic poke with the same stick.

James eyed the grey stew and poked at the lumps in some disquiet. He had read that in olden times stews were often kept simmering for weeks on end. Odd bits of meat like rabbit or vegetables were continually being added as they became available. Barnaby broke a loaf in half and offered one half to James who immediately decided that, of what was on offer, this was probably the safest option. Some sweet smelling liquid was poured into the beakers from a gourd and

Barnaby took a deep, well earned draught. After the draught he exhaled a long 'Ahh' a sound of pleasure. A sound that would change little in three thousand years. James eyed the liquid suspiciously but following reassuring gestures of encouragement from Barnaby, took a sip. It was good, very good. A cross between a cider made from pears and a spirit made from, he had no idea. James decided to be really careful, for this was probably a locally brewed, head-banging Hooch that would creep up and attack him in the back of the legs.

The meal finished, they talked for a while about life in the village and then settled down for the night, Barnaby on the stick bed and James on some rugs in front of the fire with Meg just touching him. He lay there looking up at the thatch wondering what world he had stumbled into. The whole situation made no sense to him, none at all. He reached over and ruffled Meg's ears; his only link back to the year two thousand A.D.

She wagged her tail and gave him a 'don't ask me' sort of look. James was sure she shrugged her shoulders before settling down for the night with a long sigh.

James was wakened by someone rustling about in the room. Dawn was just breaking and he could see through the loose sacking door that the first light of day was watery and unwelcoming. He propped himself up on one sore and stiff elbow and after looking at his watch exclaimed, "Barnaby, what on earth are you doing? It's not even 4.30 yet."

"I like to get an early start on the day. Not like some, lying in their beds till noon!" rebuked Barnaby. "I like to be up and about when the birds are still coughing before they start to sing. And what in the name of all the god's are 4.30?"

"It's not an are, it's an is, and it's the time."

"How do you know?"

"It's on my watch."

"Watch? What's a watch?

"It tells the time."

"It tells the time what? You said it tells the time. What does it tell the time? Why do you need a 'watch'? I get up when it's light and I go to bed when it's dark. I eat in the middle of the day when the sun is at its highest. What other time is there?" asked Barnaby flatly.

"Here, look," and with that James showed Barnaby his watch.

"I saw it yesterday on your wrist and was about to ask what measure of trinket it was when the stone slipped down into the hole and then I forgot. Show me how it works," requested Barnaby.

James slipped the watch off his wrist and handed it to Barnaby. He shook it and turned it over and suddenly exclaimed when he saw the second hand continually moving, "By all the gods it's alive!"

"No, no," explained James, "it's a mechanical watch. It runs on solar power..." James trailed off not knowing the words to use to explain. He even questioned why knowing that it was 4.30am. was so important.

They ate some bread and dried fruit and drank some watered down wine. Soon they were off to harness the horse.

As they walked alongside the cart on their way to the quarry James thoughtfully asked, "Explain exactly why you build these stone circles."

Barnaby began, "Many, many years ago, when I was just a novice priest I had a dream. I dreamt I was travelling with the gods across the universe. It was such a wonderful experience, there was no noise and there was no wind, just a sky full of shooting stars, light and brilliance. We flew close to each star in turn." And with that Barnaby spanned the whole universe with his arm as if it was night-time and every star could be seen. "On not one of those stars up there, and he arced his arm again across the sky at the invisible millions in the heavens, "was there a sign that said the gods would be welcome to visit. I watched them all sigh, one by one and ask each other the question, 'why don't people want us to visit them? Why are we not welcome? Folk put lanterns outside their doors to welcome strangers; they send invitations to friends and arrange feasts for guests. They send travellers out to meet visitors to keep them safe and show them the way to their houses, but never a sign for us'.

The gods shook their heads sadly.

'They say they leave food for us, they say they pray to us, they even sacrifice things to us but what's the value in that when we're not there to see it? Why don't they show us where to come? What is it that they are frightened of? Are we that fearsome, are we not loving gods? We want a sign that says gods, please come to visit us here. We welcome you with open arms to our village. Tarry for a while here with us, come and feast with us'.

'A simple sign would do; a line of stones guiding us to a place to stop and stay for a while; or a pile of stones, anything.'

"I watched all the gods sigh in loneliness," said Barnaby.

"When I awoke from my dream I asked the High Priest what I should do and he said 'you don't need me to tell you what to do. You already know'. He was right I did know. So, ever since that dream it has been my life's work to ensure that the next time the gods pass by they will know they're welcome here on my star and they will know where to stay. I have been placing lines of stones all around the Berwyn Mountains for the last twenty years, all pointing to the final stone circle we're building today. So that, young man, is why I spend my days building stone circles; to invite the gods," and then Barnaby went quiet.

It was true, there were lines and part lines of stones all over Wales that couldn't be explained thought James. Nobody had, to his knowledge, ever plotted them to this point on the Berwyn Mountains. Could this be the answer, a Neolithic landing strip, a sign to be seen in the heavens, a Stellar welcoming mat?

James was fascinated.

3

Today's huge stone slid silently off the steadied cart and into the hole, just as yesterday's had. It was strange, that with just two more stones the circle had been transformed from a jumble of abandoned rocks into more than half of a circle of stones. James had the same satisfaction he had experienced the previous day contributing to building a monument that would puzzle the archaeologists and historians for centuries. But now he had an explanation, a solution to the puzzle. Barnaby took time out to show the curious James the lines of stones that all pointed towards the stone circle they were building. The stone circle was like a child's picture of the sun with lines of stones as sun beams radiating across the mountains in every direction. The whole structure was immense. No wonder it had taken Barnaby so many years.

Barnaby showed James how he had erected a huge pole in the centre of the circle and then on all the adjacent mountains three shorter poles were lined up with the tall circle pole. It was easy for James to see how the centre pole could be seen up to 5 miles away. Like so many things in life it was obvious when pointed out to him.

James couldn't believe that, from the sky, the stone circle could have been missed for all this time by aerial surveys and helicopter flights. Then he wondered if many of the stones in the lines, throughout time, could have been removed for corner stones to build houses and outbuildings around the mountains for stock, their significance escaping the honest local farming folk. The only things that would have definitely been left alone were the burial sites and the stone circle for fear of spiritual retribution on the perpetrator.

Today the rain had been relentless, that wetting, Welsh rain that finds every buttonhole, every gap. Today there had only been some goat's milk cheese and bread for lunch with what rainwater they could collect. The day had been hard and the day had been long. When Barnaby suggested it was time to return home James could not have been more pleased. Despite the strange circumstances, James was beginning to like the 'old monk' and secretly admired his ability to work so hard. He questioned him endlessly about life in the current time, who was in power, who were their enemies, what were the politics, how did people trade and what were the currencies of the day?

They arrived back to consternation in the village. A crowd was waiting in the rain for Barnaby to return. In the front of the crowd a mother was sobbing and holding her limp young son out to Barnaby to heal. As soon as he saw her, Barnaby ran the last few steps throwing the reins of the horse over to James. "See to the horse," he shouted back.

James walked the tired horse over to the stable, unharnessed him, quickly brushed him down, made sure he had fresh oats and clean water and settled him for the night. He then hurried over to Barnaby's house and entered the mêlée. The mother's face was contorted in anxiety. Her hands were over her mouth holding back the huge uncontrollable sobs coming from deep, deep down close to her heart.

She had laid her small son on Barnaby's table, the very table James and Barnaby had been dining on the previous evening. The boy was aged about 6 and suffering from coughing fits. Barnaby cleared the house of all but the mother and relatives and started to wash the boy in clean warm water. The little boy went into a coughing fit that racked his whole body, brought his knees up to his chest to relieve his hurt and made every person watching, wince in sympathy, James included. As the coughing intensified the little boy's face started to turn blue, first around the eyes and then across his lips and then his cheeks. The onlookers were willing the air to get down into his lungs. Worst of all it was such a terrifying sight for the mother when her son couldn't breathe and there was absolutely nothing she could do.

Following each coughing fit the little boy calmed for a few moments. James asked Barnaby what was the matter, to be told in a whisper, 'He had a fever and his chest was closing up. He would not be with them long.' James leaned over and listened to the little boy's laboured breathing. The little boy struggled to fill his little lungs and gasped in whoops to force air into his lungs, all followed by another coughing bout that all but tore the house apart. The little boy was very ill. James kept looking from the little boy to Barnaby and back to the little boy.

Barnaby called for someone to come to the house. An old man dutifully shuffled in. After a whispered conversation he left but not before having cast a professional eye over the size of the little boy. He was the coffin maker. The little boy's mother wailed in anguish when she saw him.

James asked Barnaby what medicines were available to be told, "The only medicine now is prayer. Pray to every god you know."

"No, no, no," said James. "It's whooping cough! Kids don't die from whooping cough. It's easy to cure." Barnaby shook his head from side to side not wanting to give any indication of hope but the boy's mother had heard James and ran over to him pulling at his jacket. She pleaded with him to do something so that her helpless son wouldn't die. The mother's pleading touched James, touched him deep, deep down in places his life of materialism and wealth had long since buried.

James couldn't imagine what the woman was going through. To lose a son must be the worst torment there could be for a parent, but to watch helplessly as he died in front of you was beyond his comprehension of parental pain. He understood infant mortality rates were high in under-developed countries resulting in large families where the law of averages meant, at least some of the children, would survive to support their parents. However, with this woman no other children were evident.

James asked if Barnaby had any honey and lemon immediately realising nobody in the room had ever seen a lemon, let alone tasted one. Barnaby rummaged amongst some jars and produced a jar of honey.

"Garlic?" Barnaby's blank look said it all. James made Barnaby put a huge pot of water on the fire and stoke the fire until the pot was boiling furiously. James wouldn't leave until the steam filled the house. The boy's mother was imploring James to do something quickly.

James rushed out of the house and ran to the riverbank he'd followed with Barnaby earlier that morning. He'd smelt that distinct garlic smell when he was near the river. Stumbling along the riverside he frantically searched for wild garlic. With wet and cut hands from the brambles, he eventually trod on a bunch of the sought after plant. The wild garlic immediately released its pungent, strong, welcome smell. James dug up several cloves still attached to their soft green leaves and ran back to the house. When he threw back the sacking cloth door to the house it was just like a sauna, exactly as he wanted. "More water, more fire, more steam," James shouted at the sweating Barnaby.

James washed the garlic in some clean water and started to crush it into one of Barnaby's wooden bowls. It wasn't long before he had a ½ inch of garlic juice in the bottom of the bowl. He sieved off the solids and then to the garlic juice he added the honey and a little hot water.

James went across the steamy room to the little boy who was about to start another coughing fit. Lifting his head he spooned some of the amber juice into his mouth. The boy spluttered and tried to spit out the strange substance but suddenly realised its sweetness. The boy relented and swallowed, the liquid lined his throat and chest and the need to cough subsided. He lay there breathing shallowly but not coughing. Ten minutes later and just before the next bout of coughing, James gave the little boy another sip of the sweet medicine. The routine continued and the intervals between coughing bouts became longer and longer. Barnaby kept stoking the fire and fetching more water to make more steam. It all helped, the moist, warm air was easier for the little boy to breathe and the honey and garlic lined his chest and loosened the phlegm.

The whooping eventually subsided and the little boy relaxed the tension in his body. The anxious mother watched her boy start to breathe more easily. She turned with tears in her big frightened eyes and hugged James's arm. It wasn't necessary for her to say anything. Her wet eyes said it all. James nervously smiled back; they weren't quite out of the woods yet.

They made the little boy more comfortable on some furs, by slightly sitting him up but still on the table. James and the boy's mother stayed watching all night administering the pungent medicine; neither of them took their eyes off the little boy once. Barnaby stayed with them renewing the candles, making up the fire for more steam and helping James prepare more medicine. Several times James saw Barnaby looking at him curiously across the steamy room.

For the first time that evening, in a quiet time, James noticed the little boy's mother. He thought she must be about 25 years old but 25 years here were 25 hard years. The first thing that struck him was that she was fair, not dark like most of the other folk in the village. She had long, corn-coloured hair tied loosely behind her head by a beaded string. Her hair hung to the middle of her back, hair that she obviously brushed regularly, for the single loose strands shone silver in the candlelight. Her fair eyebrows and lashes were almost invisible and her skin was the colour of someone who had spent most of their life outside. He guessed her height to be about 5ft 5ins. She was slim with angular features, quite different from many of the villagers who were shorter and of a much stockier build.

Her worried eyes were the lightest blue, framed outside by feint crow's feet furrows brought about by the anxious circumstances. However, now the crisis had been contained, she exuded an air of calm that James believed was probably her natural demeanour.

She was most certainly a beautiful woman and James believed her elegance would have turned heads, three thousand years later, in the corridors of financial power in the City of London. She absently stroked her son's hand with long fingers; fingers he would have described as 'piano player's fingers' had it not been for the fact that it would be over two and a half thousand years before one would be invented. She wore a lightweight, faded, shift style dress, tied at the waist by a thin leather thong; the dress was made of a rough material that James couldn't identify. He assumed she had one for the summer and one for the winter, or perhaps she wore both in the harshest of winters in addition to a heavy shawl. Her feet were bare and covered in dirt and mud. He felt sure she would wear some sort of rough animal skin boot in the winter.

The steam from Barnaby's fire made beads of perspiration run down her cheeks that she wiped away with her bare forearm leaving traces of silver perspiration on the fine, blonde hairs of her arm. Every so often, she looked up at James and smiled such a thank you smile that he melted inside.

Despite all the care, the little boy drifted from waking to sleeping and back to waking a hundred times that night, but as the night wore on he became more settled. He coughed less and his breathing took on a peaceful rhythm of its own. Just before dawn, the little boy's mother let James carry her precious sleeping son home to her house on the other side of the village.

The inside of her house was neat, not like Barnaby's ramshackle bachelor house; here everything had a place and everything was in its place. James laid the little boy on his tidy bed and covered him over with his blanket. James propped his head up slightly with a rolled blanket. He turned to leave, only to be stopped by the boy's mother who reached up on her tiptoes and kissed James on the cheek. James looked down into her beautiful eyes, no longer full of tears but now full of thank you. He put his arm around her, gave her a squeeze and held her to him; together they watched the little boy sleeping and dreaming. As they watched the little boy's mother rested her tired head on James's chest and automatically he rested his head on top of hers. Close together, for a few moments, they listened to the successful outcome of an averted tragedy.

It had been an anxious night for both where the stakes for the little innocent boy had been life or death; a bond had now formed between James and the little boy's mother, a bond only possible from having lived and breathed through a crisis of such intensity. Several times through the night when he caught sight of her tired, anxious eyes he had found himself reassuringly patting her hand, assuring her that the nightmare would soon be over. James shook himself out of the dreamy world into which he had drifted, gave her a hug, automatically kissed her on the top of her head and wished her a goodnight.

As dawn was breaking over the village James walked thoughtfully back to Barnaby's house. He had to jolt himself back to reality and remind himself he was in a time zone several millennia earlier and should be thinking of returning home somehow; but she was pretty, very pretty and he had been captivated by her eyes.

Outside Barnaby's house was a rough coffin made to measure for the little boy, a chill reminder of the previous night and what might have been. James shuddered at the thought of a different ending to the night. Of having to lay the cold little boy's body in the coffin because he had lost his fight for life that night. Lost his fight for life because of James's lack of knowledge and skill. James shuddered again and moved the heavy wooden coffin around to the back of the house in case the boy's mother should come back.

4

It was evident that Barnaby had already gone for the day when James entered the quiet house, so he settled down to sleep on the rugs beside the slumbering fire. However, the events of the night kept coming back to him and he couldn't settle. Images kept waking him from earlier that night of a house full of helpless people putting all their innocent faith in three thousand year old medicine and gods, when the answers were all around them, but the simple herbal knowledge was absent. He wondered why he hadn't noticed the little boy's mother before and if it was just the crisis of the night that had attracted him to her or, if the circumstances had been different and there had been no crisis, would he have been so entranced?

James turned over and over trying to find a comfortable spot on the rugs but his mind was too active for his body so, after an hour or so, he gave up, washed, ate some bread and goat's milk cheese, drank some water, whistled Meg and went in search of Barnaby.

He found him prising a huge stone from the quarry face and arrived just in time to see the stone release its hold on the earth and surrender to Barnaby. The sweating priest turned and gave a huge grin to the clapping James who immediately clambered across to join him in Barnaby's newly learned, high five. Together with levers, timber rollers and an immense effort they loaded the stone onto the cart and started plodding off up the Old Drover's Road to the incomplete stone circle.

They talked as they walked. Barnaby wanted to know how James had known what to do with the little boy. James explained he knew the illness the little boy suffered from to be called whooping cough and it had been his mother who had all the healing skills. As a youngster he had watched his mother tend his younger sister Lucy when she developed whooping cough many years ago. Lucy had coughed and turned blue just as they had witnessed the night before with the little boy. He'd watched his mother mix the medicine and create steam in the room and witnessed the result. "I'm not clever," he confessed, "now my mother," he went on, "she was different, she was clever. She was always being called out to mix herbal remedies for folk who were sick, even in the year two thousand A.D. with all of the medical advancements she ..." His voice trailed off.

After a long quiet period as they walked Barnaby anticipated the barrage of questions bubbling under the surface before they were asked: "Her name is Eira. It means snow in Welsh. She was called Eira because her hair was the colour of snow when she was born. Over the years I've known her, she's become more and more beautiful. Eira has one son called Sion who you met last night and no, she has no husband. He died of a fever two years ago. Eira's been looking after Sion with the help of her parents ever since and doing a really good job. And yes, she is pretty, very pretty." James spluttered something about not noticing and turned away to avoid Barnaby seeing he had coloured slightly. They walked on in silence both understanding.

Today was one of those days when the old horse chose to do what he wanted rather than what was needed and the stone's irregular shape meant it didn't fall neatly into the hole. To cap it all, it started to rain; heavy rain that only stopped when they were completely soaked. When it did stop, it only stopped until the cold wind had started to dry them and when they were nearly dry, the rain started all over again. Time and time again the rain seemed to know when they were nearly dry.

Eventually, the day was over and they made their weary way down the Old Drovers Road and headed for home, horse, cart, Barnaby and James, all wet through. James had become aware that Barnaby was walking slower and more wearily than before so offered to tend the horse allowing Barnaby to get into some dry clothes the quicker.

Inside the dry stable James unharnessed the forlorn horse and spent some time drying him off with handfuls of straw. Despite his cantankerous disposition, James had started to become fond of the old horse and constantly talked to him. He made sure he had plenty of oats and fresh water for the night and eventually he closed the stable door. A thoroughly wet James trudged wearily from the rickety stable across the track to Barnaby's house.

A huge cheer met him at the door. There in front of him was Barnaby's table laid with meats, cheeses, fruits, breads, eggs and cakes many of which James had never seen before. The smell was sensational, to a man who had only eaten goat's cheese and a crust for lunch this was a feast. Many of the village people and their children who knew Eira and Sion well had crammed into Barnaby's house. It must have been a real task to keep them all quiet while James had laboured over the horse in the nearby stable. Another big cheer went up as a very surprised, but smiling, James waved to everyone. James struggled out of his wet cagoule and was led to the table by the excited children. Ducking under the green ivy and yellow barley garlands that hung from every beam, James edged himself over to the loaded table with lots of back slapping from the adults. He turned and shouted above the noise over to Barnaby, "Did you have any part in this? It must have taken all day to decorate your house."

"No, but I'm not surprised. It's a lovely village full of lovely people. You did one of them a kindness and they all want to thank you. Is that so bad?" questioned Barnaby.

"No, no, you misunderstand," shouted the smiling James above the noise, "nobody has ever done anything like this for me before, never, not since I was a kid, not even on my birthdays, it was never like this. It's fantastic, I couldn't be more pleased, and it's wonderful." There at the head of the table, which was groaning under the weight of food, was Eira. She was smiling a smile of thank you to James accompanied by an embarrassed little wave. James waved back and returned the smile.

James found out from Barnaby that one of the elder women and her husband, whose partying days had long since gone, were looking after Sion. He was progressing well and was sitting up in bed wanting to come to the party. But he was very wheezy and his mother rightly thought it best he rest.

Up until today most of the village folk had avoided any eye contact with James, having an inherent fear of strangers or anything unknown. Now it was completely different. Everyone wanted to talk to him. He was developing a wonderful feeling inside of belonging to this village.

All the partygoers ate, drank and danced through the night. There was cheering and dancing and singing, none of which meant anything to James but he joined in good-naturedly. Every so often, between the dances, James caught sight of the little boy's mother, Eira watching him from the other side of the room. She pretended she hadn't been watching him and immediately busied herself with something trivial; she was embarrassed to have been caught out. James was delighted. Those still left at dawn were either asleep or incoherent, James being both.

At 8.30 am James was awoken by Barnaby crashing about in the house. James's head banged like a drum. That innocuous pale wine that he had so carefully avoided all evening had been innocently thrust upon him towards the end of the night and in the wonderful party atmosphere he had succumbed. Just one mug he had thought, just to be sociable, just one.

Barnaby seemed to be deliberately noisier than ever mixing a potion consisting of herbs and a multitude of dried bits and bobs. James buried his head under the blanket and wanted to die. After noisily crushing the concoction in a wooden pestle and mortar and straining it, Barnaby passed the mug to the ailing James.

"What is it?" asked the percussion headed James.

"Just drink it!" said the impatient Barnaby.

James drank…

Two minutes later, following a world record breaking sprint; pee, excrement and vomit were all exiting James's body at the same time. Outside, James groaned all the way through the ordeal. Half an hour later he returned to the house to a chuckling Barnaby.

"What the hell did you give me?" rebuked James after his bowel, bladder and stomach had been emptied time and time again.

"Just something to ensure I get some work out of you today," said Barnaby still chuckling to himself.

Prior to the potion, James had decided that today, after last night's party, was going to be a day of rest, whatever day it really was. When he woke he'd felt like death and work was out of the question.

However, following Barnaby's medicine he actually felt OK now. No, he felt very good. In fact he felt terrific, no headache, no aches or pains and no lethargy. He felt as if he had woken from a full night's deep, refreshing sleep. Whatever Barnaby had concocted it really had sorted out the mother of all hangovers. After eating some bread, bacon and cheese and drinking some diluted wine, each being an absolutely no, no, after hangovers of the past, James felt very alive.

James felt positive about life and decided to clean himself up properly for the first time since he arrived. A long, hot, power-shower on the maximum setting, a liberally applied invigorating shower gel, some coconut smelling shampoo, a really close shave followed by a stinging after-shave lotion would have been the perfect start to his day. However, in the absence of all of them the water trough would have to do.

James went outside, took off his T-shirt and gave it a wash in the trough. Embarrassed, he worked out that this was its first wash since arriving over a week ago. He hung it on some branches to dry. Then he decided to wash his stiff socks and hung them on the same bush. He hopped back to the water trough over the prickly ground, looked around, saw that nobody was about and slipped out of his Rowan trousers and pants. He quickly pulled his trousers back on deciding

59

to go commando style. He washed his Kelvin Klein pants and also hung them out in the sunshine. He joked to himself that the bush looked like Widow Twankey's washroom.

James looked into the cold barrel of rainwater next to the trough and shuddered. Taking a deep breath, he forced himself to put his head and whole chest into the barrel of icy water to bring him fully round to start the day; it would be the closest he would get to a shower. In one blast he went under the breath-taking cold water. After about five seconds while he was fully submersed he felt a little tug on his Rowans. Still under the water he waited and there it was again, another little tug on his Rowans. James came up, blew water out of his mouth and snorted like a buffalo. He then ran his fingers through his long wet hair, wiped his eyes and looked around to see what had disturbed his ablutions. There, standing on his own was Eira's son Sion. He was a bit wobbly and very pale. Nevertheless, he was standing on his own and tugging at James's trousers. James lifted him up in both hands to his eye height and said, "Well, little fellow, I didn't expect to see you around for a day or two, you must be one hell of a fighter."

The boy smiled a weak smile and James gently lowered his frail, lightweight body to the ground. James smiled back, ruffled the boy's tousled hair and pulled him closer to make him feel safe. Sadly, James could still hear the boy's laboured breathing.

Not letting go of the little boy's shoulder, James looked around to check if he was on his own and his heart skipped a beat when he saw Sion's pretty mother, Eira close by.

Sion walked slowly to his mother and, as all children do, hugged her around her legs. She bent down, whispered something in his ear and he started his way home turning to wave. James vigorously returned the wave with a delighted smile.

James turned and looked straight at Eira. Conscious that he was just in a pair of Rowans and nothing else he wondered how long she had been there. This was one of those earthy times that all the senseless pumping iron in the gym had been for; all the early morning lonely miles of running, all the sensible eating and drinking were for now and he breathed in to exaggerate his physic.

Eira coyly came over to him and stood immediately in front of him, close enough to touch. Without looking up at his face, she traced her index finger seductively through the hair on his wet chest. He stood still looking down at this beautiful woman who was trying to say thank you in the most intimate way she knew how. She ran her finger down his muscled midriff as though she was counting his abs. One, two, three, four on the left side and then she traced her finger down his right side. One, two, three, four, but this time she didn't stop at four she kept tracing her finger down until it ran along his Rowan trouser belt to the buckle. She wove her index finger in and out of the dark wiry hair just above the buckle.

James threaded both of his hands under her arms to hold her. His breathing had changed to become much deeper and his chest rose and fell to a new exciting rhythm.   As his wrists brushed against her firm breasts through her thin shift, a rainbow of irrational feelings flashed and arced between the two of them. He gently drew her towards him and she took little steps forward resisting nothing. Then he kissed the fine, golden hair on the top of her head, the fine wisps of hair he had first noticed glowing silver in the candle light in Barnaby's house. She tilted her head upwards slightly and he kissed her forehead, her eyes still closed and relaxed. He kissed her nose and then for the first time she opened her big eyes.

After a long pause while she looked slowly into each of his eyes, one at a time, she kissed him full on the mouth. Still on tiptoe, she stepped forward to stand on each of his bare feet to get taller and more intimate. She was feather-light and soft to his gentle touch. Her tiny tongue teased his demanding tongue in the kiss. James was completely under her spell and responded to her every wish. They moved closer and closer, her arms now over his shoulders one clasped at the back of his neck the other weaving her long fingers through his wet hair.

James now had one arm around her waist holding her tightly to him, not letting her go and the other cradling the back of her head holding the kiss, not letting it stop. When the kiss ended and their lips parted she laid her head on his chest and he put his head on the top of her head just as they had been the other night. James ran his hand over her long, barley coloured hair with tender strokes holding her as if they had been together forever. How long they were there neither knew, how long they were there neither cared, neither wanted to break the moment.

Every one of James's heartbeats was a drumbeat exactly in sync with Eira's. Every drumbeat unfolded a new feeling like a map being unrolled before him offering him a taste what life could be like with this beautiful woman. This feeling of weightlessness, of floating on the moment, was so new to James that he relaxed savouring every new sensation. Nothing like this had ever happened before. He'd been kissed before but never like this.

After James had left the army he had drifted into a 'quite nice to be together' relationship with his partner. Not knowing anything better, the initial infatuation with a powerful woman had challenged him. Their lovemaking had been explosive but it quickly reverted to routine sex, their relationship degenerated into being, just OK. Crashing into his mind he allowed himself to admit for the first time ever that he was lonely, even when he and his partner were together, he was lonely. In this split second of what it was supposed to be like he knew his days with his partner were numbered. Now they rarely made love, they rarely kissed, she shared none of his interests and he shared none of hers. How had they ever got together? However did they think they were in love? Life was just OK with her.

Never had James and his partner's relationship been like this, as it was at this exact moment with Eira. Not even in the beginning had it been like this. Being held by someone who wanted to hold him so much, someone who wanted him so badly that he could feel it everywhere they touched, from her tiny feet through her legs up through her whole arched and stretched body to this magical, dreamy kiss.

Still holding on tightly, not wanting the moment to end, Eira was thinking similar thoughts. She had become of age with her first red moon when she was only fourteen. The only eligible man in the village at that time was about forty and after a few years together they had a son. Her life had been fair. He didn't beat her like some of the men folk beat their wives. He shared food with her when life was hard. Her husband had been a good and honest man and provided for her and Sion. He kept them warm through the winters as if he had been her father. That was it, that was exactly it; the type of love they shared had been that of a daughter for her father not as this felt now.

This was what she had dreamed about; these were the feelings she had seen in other couple's eyes. That dreamy, can't stop thinking about him, feeling. She had always known, deep down, there had to be so much more to being with someone, so much more. Someone who wanted to touch her, someone who needed her, someone who made her heart skip when she saw them. Now as she relaxed into James's hug with her head on his chest, she closed her eyes, she felt safe, she felt she belonged, she felt at home.

He was experiencing an explosion of emotions and her chest was thumping. Both knew they had just passed through a door from which there was no easy way back.

Eira and James eventually untangled themselves and she whispered: "Tonight when the work is done, come and eat with Sion and me. Bring Barnaby. When the meal is over he will understand and leave. Please come and," she paused appealing with her big eyes, "please stay."

5

The offer of food being prepared for them was such a welcome offer. Both Barnaby and James had been struggling with a particularly difficult stone and had been for three days, so the offer of real food being cooked by someone who knew the difference between a ladle and a lamb chop was a real treat. The two of them made their way to Eira's house, Barnaby carrying a gourd of wine and James a freshly caught rabbit. Neither spoke, but both knew the order of the evening. Barnaby understood what was unfolding and on one hand he didn't want this lovely woman to be hurt, for he wondered if James would one day disappear as suddenly as he had come, but on the other hand he saw the turmoil in James's eyes and felt for him.

The meal was over quickly, there being no ceremony or theatre with food and wine as James was used to. The three of them left the table and sat on upturned logs by the fire looking into the embers, each with a goblet of wine and they talked and talked. They talked about the stone circle and Eira asked Barnaby what he would do when he had finished the circle. After a while, with wet eyes that he tried to hide, Barnaby laughed and announced with many arm gestures, "When I have finished the stone circle I shall lie down exactly in the middle and dream," they all laughed.

Then James added, "When the circle is finished I will lie down in the middle and I shall sleep for a week," and after a pause added, "and so will the old horse!" And they all laughed again.

Sion stirred in his bed with the noisy laughter so they lowered their voices; a cue for Barnaby to leave.

"I will leave you young folk and make my way to my very welcome bed if you will forgive an old man." He rose stiffly, thanked Eira for the food and looking straight at James said, "And I will see you up bright and early on the morrow young fellow."

Once he was gone the house fell silent, neither knowing quite what to do.

Then Eira moved from her log seat and sat on the floor between James's legs facing the fire; her head rested on his leg. The firelight sensed magic in the moment and performed by throwing colours of orange and yellow around the house. James automatically stroked her head and she moved and mewed into his every touch. They talked, her snuggling closer to him in the warmth, hugging his leg. His body responded to her closeness and sensed every move of hers.

"I wonder what he meant when he said he would lie down exactly in the middle and dream when the stone circle was finished," James asked absently. In mid-sentence Eira turned around and kneeled up to face him, her back to the fire and the question drifted away unanswered to the corners of the dark room. As she looked intently at him, the same feelings overcame him he had felt at the water barrel earlier that day. He gently took her face in both his cupped hands and, leaning forwards, kissed her on the forehead and then on the nose and then fully on the mouth. This time it was James who demanded to be kissed and he held her once again savouring the primeval, silent language that was passing between them.

Eira suddenly freed herself from his hold, stood up, stepped back from him one step and, crossing her arms in front of her, took a handful of her shift dress in each hand and slid it up and over her head in one movement. She tossed the garment aside and waited for his reaction. Immediately, he reached out and took both of her trembling hands in his hands. His reassuring eyes took in her whole body; from her slender legs, past her fair triangle of intrigue pointing at her womanhood, on and up over her flat stomach to her firm, dark nippled breasts, evidence of a recent, young mother. James rose and took her in his arms and held her tightly to him.

She was so beautiful; he just wanted to hold her. It was the reassuring reaction she desperately needed and she sighed relaxing into him.

Eira needed to know she was still beautiful, she needed to know she was still desirable, she needed to be wanted, she desperately wanted to be loved, she desperately wanted to love. She led him backwards towards her bed undoing his shirt buttons as they went. In two minutes he lay facing her, his face nestled onto her fresh smelling hair as it tumbled across the pillow, his right arm lay over her body, gently pulling her hip towards him so that every part of their bodies that could touch, touched. There they kissed and lay revelling in a closeness that both had only dreamed of, in their loneliness, three thousand years apart. They came from different worlds, they came from different cultures but on this night their worlds became one world. This night, neither was lonely.

6

The last five stones took their toll on Barnaby. Over the next few days his steps became slower, his breathing harsher and his sleep became fitful and disturbed. James nightly quietened Barnaby's shouting and involuntary nightmare moaning and regularly spent hours through the night mopping his wet head with cool water. His yellowing, perspiration wet hair, stuck to his parchment skin and for the first time James realised he was an old, old man nearing the end of his days. Over breakfast, James regularly asked if he was OK and did he need a day's rest only to be told that he was fine and not to bother, always finishing with, 'We're nearly there.'

James watched Barnaby take longer to get out of bed each morning; he ate less and drank more wine to dull some deep-seated pain. But one morning, with only two stones to finish the circle, Barnaby couldn't get out of bed at all. His legs had all but given up on him. James called for Eira. Together they nursed him all day and the next long night and at first light it was obvious he was not long for this world. Eira tried to feed him broth but he wasn't really interested. Despite his pain, Barnaby insisted on travelling up the Old

Drover's Road to the stone circle to see it, 'just one more time'.

James and Eira made him as comfortable as they could on some furs and he travelled in style on the same worn, splintered and scuffed cart, as a hundred stones had travelled before him. The old horse seeming to know of his precious load walked slowly and avoided every pothole on the Old Drover's Road. Once there, James carefully picked up his frail old friend and carried him to exactly the centre of the circle settling him on the furs, just as he had requested.

Together, James and Eira watched Barnaby dream his last dream ever...

Two days later Eira, Sion, James and Meg stayed and watched the embers die down from the funeral pyre in the centre of Barnaby's, nearly complete, stone circle. The whole village came to pay their respect to the old priest and in their own individual ways, said goodbye. As the fire died down and dusk began to fall so the villagers, along with Sion and Meg, made their way back home down The Old Drover's Road.

James and Eira stayed to watch the last sparks drift heavenwards in the evening breeze, believing that each spark was a part of Barnaby's spirit on its last journey up to meet the gods. The thought offered them both some comfort. When they were satisfied there was nothing left they headed homewards down the mountain. Home? Where was that James wondered? Three thousand years in the future or here in the Late Bronze Age village of Llandrillo? Who knew? What he did know was he had just lost one of the closest friends he had ever known and it hurt.

James stayed on in Barnaby's house and dealt with the steady stream of cuts, bruises, whooping cough, broken arms and all manner of ailments he had never come across before. He saw rickets and worms and all forms of malnutrition and was at a loss as to how to treat them. He was becoming recognised as the physician for the village and felt uncomfortable with his scant memories of his mother's remedies. James's inadequacies were eating at him like a sore; he felt such a fraud amongst a village of wonderful people who deserved someone more competent than himself. He vowed he would never allow himself to feel so inadequate again.

Then one day Eira called in to see James, only to find him soaking some stale bread in weak wine to make it soft enough to chew. She looked at James and found a sad man who had recently lost a friend. James was looking after himself badly. Without asking, she rolled up his bedding, packed his things and led the compliant James to her house. There she bathed him and set him up with some clean, village made clothes and spread before him a meal fit for a king. That night James felt he belonged again, he was really home and this was where he wanted to be.

The next day with Eira's energy James felt re-motivated. He harnessed the old horse, led him to the quarry and loaded the penultimate stone. He had decided to finish Barnaby's stone circle. He and the old horse laboured for the next week as he had been taught. Then the last hole was dug, the last stone quarried, the last heavy journey made and suddenly, it was finished, it was complete, the two sides of the circle had joined.

James threw down the rude shovel, wiped his brow and looked up at the sky wondering if Barnaby could see that what he had started all those years ago had now been finished. The Moel Ty Uchaf stone circle had become a legacy to Barnaby's vision and hard work, a monument to his tenacity and courage. James felt privileged to have known such a man and imagined Barnaby travelling around the stars with the gods directing them to his very own stellar sign. Barnaby would laugh that it had been finished and bring his gods to this place where he knew they would be welcome.

Now that the stone circle was complete James spent the next few months walking and talking with Eira. He avoided his past and she had the good sense to avoid it too, just in case she discovered something she didn't like and had to make decisions. She taught him about their religions, rulers, customs and history. She taught him about their traditions like marriage and naming children. She also taught him about very practical things like how she kept the flies off her when she was tending the livestock by sewing sprigs of mint into the collar of her shift dress. James hated the flies and would do anything to be rid of them.

Together they walked in every direction from the village, but their favourite place was sitting close together way above the village, watching the sun go down over the mountains on the other side of the valley. They sat together on a huge stone called Sedd y Cawr or the 'giant's seat'. Here was their very private world and here they were as happy in silence as they were talking.

In their more serious moments Eira told him of the other side of life in Llandrillo. The side of life that wasn't always as idyllic as it was right now in the summer time with a plentiful supply of food and warm weather. Right now, life was safe in Llandrillo but she assured him it could become a different place very quickly. To give him an example she showed him the small cave entrance, only big enough for a child to enter, near the giant's seat where the village children hid when the Pobl Hunllef y Dydd came, the 'Day Nightmare People' shortened to The Hunllef. The Hunllef were a wandering tribe who raided villages when they were in the area killing, raping and taking away food and livestock. They rounded up children to bulk up their tribe as slaves. Each warrior was heavily tattooed to be more frightening. Life itself had no value to the Hunllef and the village farming folk were no match for these fighting men who had been born into a world of warring. She told James the Hunllef had no society, no rules, no tomorrow. They took what they wanted and if they were resisted they killed indiscriminately. James shuddered at the thought of these lovely, gentle people living in fear of the Hunllef.

"When do they come?"

"Who knows? Sometimes we get a warning from other ravaged villages, sometimes we don't. As soon as we hear they're coming we run to the forests and hide and the children run up here to the cave behind Sedd y Cawr."

James shuddered.

She told him of their winters and the snow and ice and the hunger when the river was so cold it froze over for weeks. She tried to describe illnesses that raged through the village that seemed to have no cure. She told him of the number of children that never saw their second birthday and how last year the village folk had watched their livestock die one by one with swollen bellies and tongues that turned blue and nobody knew why. It had taken a whole year to trade with other villages to restock their pens. Life could be very cruel to Llandrillo folk.

However, more often than not, James and Eira's evenings were wonderful occasions full of closeness and togetherness. Together they watched the rolling clouds, painted scarlet by the setting sun, imperceptibly turn orange. As the evening darkened in preparation for the night, Eira and James would sit in silence and watch the heavy orange clouds transform into wispy clouds and don their nightdresses of pale pink. And then it would be dark.

Hand in hand they would walk back to the village in the moonlight stopping to hug and kiss as lovers do. Never had he been so contented with somebody, never had he felt so at ease with life, never had he been so in love. He needed to constantly be close to her. He found he couldn't pass her without touching her. Whenever he was within distance he would reach out and run his fingers across her back or hold her tiny waist to squeeze past in her small house. Every time they were close by they both leaned towards each other to kiss.

Outside, every night before they went to bed, their routine was to look up at the night sky for shooting stars that Barnaby might be riding upon. He would wrap his arms around her from behind and hold her tightly, she in turn would let her head fall back and rest on his chest and together they watched the night sky. They were so happy.

Eira wanted to spend every moment with James. From the time she opened her eyes and smiled watching and hoping to silently wake him, to the time they held each other closely and said a prayer to each other to stay safe through the night. Her heart leapt with delight when he returned home early from helping someone less fortunate than herself. And every time she woke to find herself alone in the bed she jumped out anxiously to find him preparing some poultice or potion. She would hug him hello and good morning. In return he would put his arm around her and draw her as close as he could and smile good morning back to her.

Eira also understood that her son needed the guiding hand of a father figure, someone whom she trusted. Not a figure that Sion would cower away from as did some of the village children from the men folk but a figure to whom he could look up. Eira's mother and father lived next door and did what they could to raise the boy, but their age prevented them from fulfilling the role effectively. James respectfully and affectionately adopted the names that Sion called them of Nain and Taid, grandmother and grandfather. They were a kindly pair and this was born out by the role they played in the village. It seemed to James that they gathered up all of the children and looked after them while their parents were working in the fields or out hunting; a Late Bronze Age crèche. In return, they were rewarded in grain or bread or meat. The whole society worked together; it was wonderful. James wondered how the year two thousand AD had managed to lose so many society values.

James spent the days when he and Eira weren't together teaching Sion all the things she dreamed someone would teach her son. James taught him how to tickle trout, catch squirrels and birds. He taught him how to play conkers and tie knots. He taught him how to whistle using just his fingers and Sion quickly became more proficient than James. In the evenings they wove willow tubes together to trap the salmon that moved silently in the river shadows. They tramped the fields together talking and laughing. James had been taught all of these things by his father and the army and was pleased to be able to pass then on to Sion. James taught him everything he knew about the countryside and they became very close.

Over the summer and autumn Sion grew stronger by the day by eating a balanced diet of all the right foods directed by James. Gradually Sion's chest strengthened and he started to run for the first time ever.

James taught the boy the names of all of the stars and explained how their shapes led to their names. Soon Sion could point to the Great Bear, the Plough and the North Star where ever he was and whatever the time of night. He taught him how to make owl noises to which the night always responded. He taught him how to train Meg and she reacted to the little boy's commands as if she knew how important it was for him.

But most of all he taught him how to carry on the traditions of making a stone circle. James taught him the reasons Barnaby had made the stone circle and then he taught him how. James mused that Barnaby would have been proud of him. He started on small stones and slowly moved up to bigger and bigger stones. He taught him how to harness the horse and how to make him go forward and to stop and go backwards, just as Barnaby had showed him not so very long ago. Occasionally, Eira would catch sight of the pair of them laughing as they trudged home after a hard day working on a stone circle and she would smile. She had decided to take life just one day at a time.

Sion learned quickly, he was a sponge to new skills and new thoughts. He responded to the attention of someone who wanted to teach him what some of the other children could already do. He wanted to please; he wanted to show that the time teaching him had been well spent. When he achieved a new skill he revelled in James's praise; when he got it wrong he laughed at his clumsiness and slowness and that only caused him to double his resolve. Sion brought things he had made to James for approval and when he caught a rabbit or fish it wasn't to his mother he ran but to James. James delighted in the closeness.

Then suddenly one day James realised what he was doing. He was preparing to leave!

It struck him like a thunderbolt. He was imparting all of his knowledge so that one day he could return to Barnaby's stone circle to sleep in the hope of returning to his old life in the future. Three thousand years in the future. He had been passing on to Eira everything he knew about tending the sick that could be of use in the village and teaching Sion skills to make their harsh life more bearable.

James had chopped enough wood to last them for two winters. He had rebuilt their house and Nain and Taid's with an outer layer as extra insulation ready for the winter. He had diverted the stream to bring clean water into the village and taught the village folk about sanitation.

His biggest project had been to convince the men folk of the village to help him dig a covered-in tunnel from the centre of the village out to beyond the tree line, about fifty yards. The covered-in tunnel was to enable the children to escape in the event of the Hunllef entering the village without warning. Once he mentioned the dreaded Hunllef the men folk needed little persuasion. Where the ground was very rocky the covered-in tunnel was only about five feet deep and covered in stout branches and clods of soil and grass. Where the roof would hold it was about seven feet deep. It started inside Nain and Taid's house, where the village children were most likely to be and it ran very close to the back of some of the other houses, under the fields and up into the forest where the exit couldn't be seen from the village. When it was finished and the grass had grown over, it was impossible to see there had been any disturbance.

James was happy in the village but his old life kept niggling at the back of his mind. When he left in the year two thousand he had been an ambitious financial trader in the City of London and was about to be promoted to CEO of the company. He had a dream of a house in Marlow in Buckinghamshire, which had been slowly becoming a reality, with or without his partner. His life style was comfortable, he went to the gym when he wanted, had his own P.A. and a huge office. When he travelled, he flew everywhere Business class. He never thought about money, it was never an issue. His ideal would have been to take Eira and Sion back with him but that wouldn't have been fair on either of them. Corporate life was difficult enough when one had been brought up in it, to be thrust in from a world that had just discovered the wheel was beyond comprehension.

Back home, James drove a top-of-the-range Aston Martin and belonged to the best golf club in the British Isles. His friends were challenging and quick witted. They were equally ambitious in their own fields. He enjoyed their company, banter, competitiveness and humour. That was what he missed most, the challenge and the humour of his friends. But that was where his yearning ended; his friends had huge overdrafts and a laissez-faire attitude towards the plight of folk less fortunate than themselves.

They broadly fell into two different groups; there were the aquaholics; those rich guys who bought bigger and better yachts than their friends. The sailing fraternity, who owned the boats, talked incessantly about sailing but couldn't sail without a paid-for skipper and crew. They described their sport as 'standing under a cold shower tearing up £50 notes'. Then there were the airoholics, James's flying friends who had learned to fly, bought a small plane, bought a bigger plane, bought a small jet or chopper, flew it for a short time and when the aircraft needed servicing had to sell the jet or chopper to pay for the service.

Most of his friends were also petroholics, owners of fancy cars that were completely impractical for today's roads, didn't have room enough for two shopping bags and uncomfortable as hell. James excused his Aston as his only toy. He didn't miss his friends' shallowness.

He found himself having more and more of these mind debates and came to the conclusion that the outlook on life of most of his friends was superficial. Their way of life had none of the richness he shared with these village people. Despite all of their obscene salaries his friends somehow managed to exceed their incomes in a race for more and still more. There was nothing his friends had or, indeed he had, that was better than his village friends had now.

For instance, the first cry of a baby was as special an experience where he was now as it ever was to be three thousand years later; each time he heard it in the village it brought a lump to his throat and tears to his eyes. The smell of freshly baked bread in the morning never changed. The sight and smell of oats and barley blowing gently in the evening breeze like fur; the morning sun and the night sky was as spectacular here as it was ever going to be three thousand years later. The touch and caress of a woman who loved you so deeply that it hurt would never change in its intensity however many millennia it spanned.

What was it again that was so wonderful about the time he had left behind he kept asking himself? Maybe unachieved financial ambitions, maybe unachieved personal goals, maybe unachieved physical targets, he couldn't fathom out the dilemma, but somehow there was an inexplicable draw.

James tried to understand what he missed. Was it that he was anxious not having access to doctors and medicines, medicines as insurance against illnesses that might come his way? A perfectly reasonable anxiety he argued. However, after much thought he decided that most of the medicines he wanted to have access to were to cure the societal illnesses of the year two thousand AD - HIV, cancer, heart problems and many others - not the medicines to fulfil the needs of these village folk and their illnesses. He concluded after much thought he really didn't need the medicines that made him anxious about their absence. Arguments like these ranged back and forwards in his mind.

Thankfully, here there was no oil. Here there was no petrol or diesel. Thankfully, here there was no greed for the wealth that drove men to lie and cheat and fight for ownership of the black gold. Here, in the year one thousand BC there was a simple life where honesty and integrity were the corner stones of this society and whole families were welcomed or shunned by their attitudes towards their neighbours. Initially, when groups of houses formed into a village, tough pecking orders needed to be established, jealousy and rivalry was quickly stamped out and normal village life prevailed. Here, village folk fought against nature for their very survival not against each other for bigger houses and more expensive watches.

A watch, what a complete and utter waste of space that invention was. The best timepieces in the world were the sun during the day and at night, the moon. And he had wondered how he could possibly manage without a watch when he first arrived. It took an old priest to embarrass him by listening to his fumbled explanation of its importance. And now it had hung limply on a peg in Eira's house for three seasons.

But, here he had happiness, here he had love, here was a world where he was needed in fact, constantly in demand, in demand for things that really mattered in life. Disputes were set out before him to arbitrate between families. Land arguments were brought before him to be settled as they had been with Barnaby before him. He was asked to interpret the signs of the gods which he did with due reverence to their culture. The lack of rain, which was seen as the only source of water for the crops, was supplemented by water from the diverted stream as well as praying to the rain gods. An outbreak of diarrhoea was reversed by simple good hygiene practices as well as offering appeasements to the gods. Never once did he despair at their primitive answers to problems or naivety but sensitively found solutions that solved their problems and also supported their beliefs. James became well respected in the community, as did Eira for all her healing capability.

On top of all the arguments whether to go back or stay, James angst over whether it would still be the same time back in the future or would time have moved on. Could it be if he slept against the stone again he would wake up at some arbitrary time say, five hundred years from now, or five hundred years even earlier? Then he would have lost Eira, Sion and his job in the City.

If he did get it right, would his place still be open in the financial sector where he had fought so hard to establish himself? Would there be someone else's name on his door, someone else sitting in his office at his desk? He knew there were a hundred, hungry young financial Turks watching his every corporate move, all baying for his job at the slightest sign of weakness; and absence was a sign of weakness. Or would time have stood still and he would return to exactly the same hour and time that he left? The stakes were very high in this decision. Many hours of sleeplessness were to follow.

7

Having finally made his decision to go back, the evening came for him to leave, exactly one year to the day since he arrived, the summer solstice. James kept everything as normal as possible although Eira had recently sensed a slight change in him and his demeanour. Each night she held him a little bit closer in case the worst should happen and he would leave to mend some poor soul without waking her. That evening Sion had long since gone to bed and the two of them sat in the fire light without speaking as close as they could be, just as they had done a hundred times before.

Eventually, they settled for the night. James could not be more awake. He lay as still as he could, a warm rosy glow surrounded them in those last precious moments. He smelt her hair and held her naked body as close as he could to him. Memories he wanted to be able to recall when he wouldn't be able to touch her. Slowly but surely her breathing became rhythmical and he gently eased himself away from her. Twice she moved in her sleep and edged closer to him, her soul and the gods combining all their efforts, willing her to wake and stop him from going.

He obliged and held her again, she relaxed trusting him and all of the doubts came crashing back to him. Here he was safe; here he was loved with a love he was sure he would never find again. But the pull of the future tugged at him and once again he slowly eased himself out of the bed.

James's dog Meg had become so fond of Sion that they were never apart. She slept at the foot of Sion's bed with one paw over the boy's leg just as she had done with James. They had become inseparable. James moved towards the boy's bed and ruffled the dog's ears and gestured for her to stay. She seemed to understand and rested her head back on his blanket. There would be too much heartache in this household in the morning for the boy to lose his dog as well. James placed his coveted Swiss army knife on the small shelf next to the boy's bed and moved back across to Eira's bed and watched her even breathing. He carefully lifted the covers and watched her lithe naked body rise and fall with each breath, she was so beautiful; what on earth was he doing? He leant down and just touched her head with his lips and kissed her. A wisp of her hair was across her nose and he brushed it off her face as gently as if he were stroking a butterfly wing.

And then he was gone. Out into the chill night air pacing off to the circle. It took a good 40 minutes to reach to stone circle up the Old Drover's Road and when he arrived at the circle he was out of breath. He walked up to the very stone where he had fallen asleep a year ago to the day and slid down its polished surface. Facing inwards he looked around in the moonlight and up at the stars and said out loud to the absent priest, "You were right Barnaby, it really is the most beautiful place in the world."

James had no idea when he would wake could it be he was going back to the right time 2000 AD, or even further back to 3000BC. Might he wake in Roman Britain as a slave or the Middle Ages as a merchant? What a risk he was about to take.

He allowed his eyes to slowly close and soon he was slumbering. He was in that half-land between sleep and now, when a noise behind him brought him back from his dreaming. He stood up and looked around to see Sion standing there with a panting Meg. James and Sion stared at each other for what seemed like an age before Sion spoke stoically with tears streaming down his face.

"You left your dog," and with that Sion handed James the lead, turned and started back down the mountain without looking back.

8

James came to slowly and realised where he was; nothing had changed from when he left a year ago to the day. The Berwyn Mountains were exactly as he had left them. The stone circle was complete with its 41 stones, exactly as he had left it when he first went to sleep. There was no charring in the centre of the circle from Barnaby's funeral pyre. He looked around to see if the last thing he had seen was still there, Sion, and was filled with disappointment when the boy was nowhere to be seen. James was still wearing his cagoule and walking boots. He rose up from the stone and checked his rucksack. It still contained his second sandwich wrapped in its unopened tin foil wrapping. Could he have dreamt it all? Barnaby, Eira, Sion, Nain and Taid. Could it all have been just a vivid dream? It must be the only explanation.

He had dreamt everything. He had dreamt the whole thing, everything. The time was 12.30pm about 30 minutes from when he'd fallen asleep. Meg was bounding around the circle smelling every stone just as she had before he went to sleep. The mountains were the same, the sky was the same, it was now daylight and even the stones were the same. James took off his cagoule and draped it over one of the stones as the sun was at its highest and now warmer than ever. Then he spotted it sewn into his cagoule collar…

A sprig of mint!

9

Beth strained her neck to see along the queue of visitors to see how far it went. The queue stretched as far back as the car park. Four coach parties of Japanese had arrived at the Stonehenge Heritage site at the same time. Four coaches amounted to about 240 visitors, all to be given tickets and directions. Beth flippantly wondered if Japan was empty today for the population was all here! Stonehenge was a fabulous heritage and she could not be more proud of the site, but for them all to arrive at the same time was ludicrous. Surely it wasn't beyond the wit of the coach companies to stagger the arrival of so many visitors. Hanging her grumbles up with her jacket she opened the kiosk window and offered a smiling welcome to each visitor in turn, directed them to where they could obtain an audiotape and wished them a pleasant day.

She considered herself so lucky to have secured a job, however menial, working at such close quarters to her beloved Stonehenge. Ever since she had been a little girl she had been fascinated by the whole intriguing concept of stone circles; ancient folk building such wonderful legacies, five thousand years ago. She had pursued her interest through secondary school and on to university where she had read Neolithic history obtaining a First. So good had her research been that she had immediately been invited to undertake her Masters on the subject. On completion of her Masters, which she saw as her hobby rather than study, she was invited to continue for her PhD. Her parents had been financially stretched to send her to university in the first place and encouraged her to stay on for her Masters, but another three years was out of the question so she had looked for a job close to her passion in life and here she was, a ticket sales girl at Stonehenge.

Beth was now in her third year of the PhD and challenging much of the established thinking. She was also rocking some of the Stonehenge theories of eminent historians of the last three centuries. Living as she had as a child, teenager, young adult and now doctoral researcher amongst the stones, she had developed a feel for them. She had developed an understanding of their meaning, their moods, of their very reason for being here. As far as she could tell in recent history there was nobody who had spent as much time with the stones as she had. With that familiarity had developed empathy, Beth felt for the ancient majestic centre of ritual as it was surrounded by yet another daily endless snake of sightseers. The stone's longevity and impressive stature paid little heed to the visitors but to Beth they were not being awarded their proper recognition. Her anger had exploded on several mid-summer's nights in the past when the stones had been climbed upon and defaced by partying Hippies. She had been escorted away by security on two occasions and now she chose to stay away, the experience was too painful for her.

Now that her research had reached an advanced stage, what Beth was not prepared to do was wait until the current thinkers with their intransigent views had died, before challenging their thinking. Consequently, she was beginning to make herself thoroughly unpopular with the academic establishment. Beth's early theories flew in the face of John Aubrey's (1626-1697) thinking. The 17th century antiquarian had formed the basis of all Stonehenge thinking for three centuries.

The queue of visitors slowly but surely reduced in size despite a further coach load and 290 visitors wandered on their noisy, camera flashing walks around the circle.

Near the end of the queue stood a guy in his early thirties reading as he queued. Beth established he was on his own and not too pleased by the long wait. She was intrigued by this single, good-looking visitor and couldn't wait for him to get to the front. Eventually he was there. The book he was reading was entitled 'Standing with Stones' written by Rupert Soskin. Beth instantly recognised the book as one of the best and most revered books on standing stones ever written. Excitedly she asked, "Enjoy the book?"

"Yes, nearly had time to read it from cover to cover this morning," replied the good-looking visitor, sarcastically responding to whom he considered to be just someone who sold tickets to see the stones.

Ignoring the justified sarcasm Beth asked, "What was your best bit of the book? Was it the photos of the circles that captured your imagination or the author's exposition on their origins of standing stones? Which site intrigues you the most? Is it the enormous ring of Brodgar or the complex sprawling Avebury?" James was taken aback by the swiftness of her reply to his sarcasm and immediately recognised he had completely misjudged this woman.

An early start from London to ensure he was at the site by 8.45am was thwarted when he queued in his Aston Martin behind a coach to enter the Stonehenge car park. He had groaned out loud and spun his car noisily into the car park to get in front of the coach passengers. He had been feeling good that he'd parked first and quickly walked past the coach before it had time to disgorge its occupants, only to be met by the end of the queue of 200 passengers from coaches he hadn't seen. James decided coffee was a good alternative to queuing so he sat out the first four coach loads and joined the last. Having been asked countless times if 'You take photo please?' by the Japanese visitors he had buried his head in his book and shuffled forwards ignoring any further requests. Regrettably, he was not in the best of moods and the woman inside the kiosk had taken the brunt of it.

James dutifully handed over the fee and requested a guidebook as a memento. Intrigued, he decided to test the woman and said, "My favourite site is Moel Ty Uchaf. Know it?"

"Yes, about two miles from Llandrillo up on the Berwyn Mountains. 41 quite small stones but their size, rather than lessening the circle's grandeur, only add to its elegance. Have you ever been there at sunset because if you haven't, I highly recommend it?" said Beth smugly, now not liking this visitor one bit. Without looking up she followed her exact description of Moel Ty Uchaf with a curt, "Next."

James was not used to being put in his place but he had been on this occasion with her exact description of Moel Ty Uchaf. He had also been summarily dismissed when she had said, 'Next'.

The stream of visitors slowed to a trickle and apart from the middle-aged couple who became very upset when Beth tried to sell them two OAP's tickets the morning went without incident. The woman was enraged and demanded an apology from Beth for the error. Beth only made things worst by trying to explain that she was sorry for the error but the scratches on the kiosk window gave everyone a wrinkled look. Behind the back of the irate woman the woman's husband winked at Beth, ran his finger across his throat in the form of an apology and pointed at his wife. Beth acknowledged him with an embarrassed smile.

Beth had worked at Stonehenge for two years now and spent all her spare time and days off walking beneath the majestic stones. She walked at every time of the day. She came early in the morning to watch the sun rise, she stayed late at night to watch the sun set, she even came back at night and walked amongst the stones in the mist and dew. Here, she believed there was a long lost order to life set out in the arrangement of stones; here there was a pattern superimposed on the visual pattern of stones; here there was a secret.

With instruments she had surveyed the henge from every angle, at every time of the day and night. But the time she felt closest to the secret was at night. Now she had the makings of a theory developing in her head. She believed she was looking at the vague answer, like looking through a misty, lace curtain at images beyond, willing her to come through. She was now convinced the stones were arranged to follow other cycles, the summer solstice cycle being just too obvious for such an advanced people.

Her part-time PhD had been paid for, so far, by a massive student loan, her pay from the kiosk, birthday presents and Christmas presents of money. So far, she was OK with the finances; she lived frugally and ate vegetarian, meat being a luxury. As soon as her relief arrived at the kiosk Beth picked up her plastic lunch box and wandered off to her special spot looking directly at the stones.

James listened intently to the audiotape but his mind wandered back to the woman in the kiosk. She had fascinated him, so much so, that when he had circled the stones twice, knew every word of the audiotape off by heart, he went off in search of her. She was the first person he'd ever met who had even heard of Moel Ty Uchaf. He was really disappointed to be told she had already left to have lunch.

"Anyone know where she has lunch?"

"Over there by the ditch, same place every day."

"Thanks."

James bought himself a sandwich and a coffee and walked across towards the kiosk woman."

"May I join you?"

Beth looked up, "Be my guest, Grumpy."

He settled next to her introduced himself and took up the conversation.

"Hi, I'm James and I deserved that. Sorry."

"Beth, and your apology is accepted."

"So tell me, how did you get interested in standing stones?"

While she explained he looked at her properly for the first time. She was about 5ft 9ins, late twenties, slim with shoulder length, dark brown hair. The top of her head had some of her hair coloured auburn by the sun and it was fresh, clean, recently washed and the light wind lifted the ends. She carried no extra weight and her complexion was perfect as were her teeth. Her clothes were typical student clothes, long lasting and washed many times. Her jacket was faded matching her jeans, but what captured his attention was her smile. She looked at him and smiled a smile that made him think there was much, much more to this woman. Because, beneath her smile there was an anxiety that he couldn't understand; James was intrigued by her, all his sarcasm disappeared, all his self-importance shelved, he liked her.

She began: "When I was a little girl I was brought here kicking and screaming by my grandfather. I didn't want to see any mouldy old stones, I wanted to go shopping or the cinema or go and listen to music with my friends. But when I saw them for the first time, 'Wow'. I just stood amongst them speechless. They were magnificent, tall stones, set in arches that I was allowed to walk beneath. My grandfather talked as we walked around the stones.

"He told me each stone had a story to tell; where it had come from, how it had travelled, incidents on the long journey and how, one day, he believed they would all go home. He couldn't say how or when, but my grandfather was sure one day they would all make the journeys back home. There were no audiotapes in those days; there were no pamphlets, no guidebooks. Just the stones and he said, 'Beth darling, whatever began in the year 5000 B. C. will never end, for nobody will ever be able to untangle the true meaning of the stones, their reason for being or what we can learn from them.'"

"Well, this was like throwing down the gauntlet. I wanted to prove my grandfather wrong. I would understand the stones, me Beth… And the rest, as they say, is history."

Beth stopped talking and looked across at her beloved stones. She continued with, "Now I love this place so much it's where I get my 'awe-therapy', that wonderful state you feel when you see something so beautiful, so amazing you're left in a state of peace. When I'm here, I'm grounded, I'm peaceful, I exist in a waiting state continuing my researching so that one day I'll be able to reveal the true story of the stones. I'm very happy."

James listened fascinated by her and asked, "How do you know about Moel Ty Uchaf?"

"Oh, I don't," she admitted, "I've just read the book from cover to cover a dozen times and know it off by heart," and she looked at him and laughed. James laughed too.

"And I was thinking you'd been there."

James believed here was someone who would listen with an open mind if he told her his story of Moel Ty Uchaf but before he said a thing he would need to be sure.

"What time do you finish?"

"Six."

"Could we go somewhere to eat?"

"Sure."

"Pick you up here at six then."

"Great."

With that she threw the last of the crumbs to the hopping sparrows, clicked her plastic lunch box shut, shouted 'Bye, see you at six,' and left.

James spent the rest of the day either sitting in the Aston conducting business, which had been installed with as much equipment as his office, or in the sunshine reading the collection of new books he had just bought from the Stonehenge shop.

However, his mind kept drifting back to his stone circle, Moel Ty Uchaf and all the things he needed to learn before returning to Eira's world. Only days into 2000 and he knew he had got it all wrong, he was now in the wrong place. He needed to go back, already he missed her. He had met up again with the friends he believed he would have missed and he wouldn't have swapped any of them for Nain or Taid. He had re-tasted the corporate world and now it held little intrigue. Despite all he had promised himself he would learn in the year in preparation for his return he vowed he would still try to visit a circle every month and today was Stonehenge's turn. However, it didn't hold the same fascination of Moel Ty Uchaf. Perhaps Beth could help him to see beyond the tourism, new road systems and coach parks.

10

Professor Brendon Quail unscrewed the lid of the bottle of tablets cursing the totally unnecessary childproof lid and his clumsy fingers. He emptied two tablets into his hand and threw them to the back of his throat; cold coffee washed them down. He was now on double the recommended dose of painkillers per day and rued the day he had ever stepped foot in South America to study the indigenous stone structures. His pain came from a tropical disease that was slowly eating away at his organs. His incontinence restricted all of his movements, he could only work from his office now, he couldn't travel and worst of all it was terminal. Now he had the date, twelve months at the present rate of deterioration.

Professor Brendon Quail was a slight man with pointed features, a Dickensian, shrew-like character whose lack of zest for life was matched only by his meanness. His career had moved slowly, by attendance only, up through the hierarchy of the university positions from a part-time researcher up to professor, but it had taken forty-four years. He had moved to another university for a short time but quickly returned when it became apparent to his new employers that his knowledge was predominantly second hand. His spiteful demeanour and underhanded dealings left him with few friends.

Despite his lack of original research he had a dream, an impossible dream. Before he died his dream was to leave a legacy to the human race that had his name on it, The 'Brendon Quail Theory', a theory that would shake the whole academic world. It would be a theory that would be taught in the best universities in the world, an exposition that would be the envy of all of his colleagues. The focus he had chosen for the 'Brendon Quail' exposition was Stonehenge. Only then would he have fulfilled his life's ambition, to be recognised.

His life's research work to date had amounted to little more than some spurious research into Neolithic house design and some theories about Neolithic social structures and these had been met with only a lukewarm reception from the accepted body of eminent brains at 'Conference'.

Being completely immobilised by his illness the professor's only hope now was to piggy-back on some rising star in the field. He had been told of the work that was being undertaken by a bright new student researching at Stonehenge for her PhD. He remembered her name as one of those women students who scorned his attentions nearly ten years ago, early on in her career. He remembered being hit by her when he suggested an, 'arrangement' to raise her grades. He rubbed his jaw in painful memory. However, she seemed to be thinking differently from the conservative dogma and she may even have forgotten the incident. He had tracked her down, followed her progress and decided she was clever, very clever, for she had shared only snippets of her research in various published journals whetting the reader's appetite. The academic world did not like new thinking, for it demonstrated they had missed things in their research. It demonstrated that their calculations had been, using generous criticism, misguided and, using less charitable language, wrong!

Try as he might, he could not find out what exactly she was researching and short of declaring an interest and talking to her direct he was at a loss as to how to gather the information. In desperation he had enlisted some assistance, through a third party of course, for he wanted no contact with her at all. He wanted to be able to present her work and findings at 'Conference' as his own with complete conviction and be able to say with honesty that he had not met, or spoken to, the young lady since she was an undergraduate.

Professor Brendon Quail had, through this third party, secretly employed the five security guards who looked after the Stonehenge site day and night, to diary all her movements and photograph any of her documents and drawings. They were to report on the exact positions she stood in amongst the stones, what time of day or night it had been and what she did next. All of the five weekly diaries were to be sent to a PO Box and anything urgent was to be telephoned immediately to an answering service.

There had to be no audit trail that could lead back to him.

So far, she had been recorded spending much of her time at night at one of three locations in the inner circle. From the information communicated by the security guards he had plotted the frequency of her positions and felt sure she was on to something. Due to being desk bound he had to replace personal visits to Stonehenge with the diaries of the five security guards and feed their information into the huge assortment of computer power available to him at the university. With all this computer power he had calculated every option from the diaries. The computers had come up with... nothing.

He now had all of her movements for the previous nine months... but he didn't have her thinking, he didn't have her intuition.

11

The restaurant recommended to James by Beth stood opposite Salisbury Cathedral's West gate in a commanding position and served food that was every bit as good as the French menu described. Beth hadn't been taken out for dinner for a very long time and hesitantly asked if it was OK to order the steak. Steak was a luxury she hadn't tasted for a very long time. James smiled and said, "Be my guest," and ordered some wine after checking with her. He found her easy to talk to, she was fresh, herself and not covered in make-up trying to be somebody she was not. Her hair wasn't dyed, her fingernails were natural and she wore no make-up. She didn't need paint or powder; she had that wonderful vitality of youth instead. They laughed together when the waitress brought out the bread sticks with the drinks. They had to be approaching two feet long, a credit to the chef's steady hands. Beth declared 'she had never eaten a yard of bread before'.

Their conversation flowed warmly and easily, eventually drifting back to the stones.

"How can anyone not be in awe of the stones?" Beth asked.

"How can anyone see them or be close to them and not feel inadequate amongst these enduring symbols of mystery? How can anyone stand near them and not be blown away by the size of the sarsen stones? Do you know some of them weigh more than 40 tons, dragged all the way from the nearest source in Wiltshire about 40 miles? They make up the trilithons, two huge uprights capped by a sarsen lintel. Most engineers today wouldn't have the foggiest clue how to raise the lintels up that high. The bluestone's story is even more amazing. The bluestones were transported by ship and sledge all the way from the Preseli hills in Wales about 150 miles? How incredible is that? We'd think twice about transporting them even now.

"Not only are they a magnificent group of stones but also they're arranged in a really sophisticated alignment. It's so sophisticated that we can't even work it out now with all our 'so called' advancements. We think we have but we haven't!"

James just listened.

Beth was in her element, "The stones have been many things in their lifetime James. A burial site for laying to rest the cremated bones of 60 young men. Why? We don't know why, we haven't got a clue! We think we're smart but we're not. Did you know that healing properties were attributed to the blue stones? They're supposed to have fertility properties as well, but thank God that seems to be a myth as I've spent years in amongst them and nothing has happened so far. There are even legends that suggest if a maiden walked through the trilithons then she would become more attractive to men. That's a myth too 'cos I'm still single." Beth laughed out loud and then realised she was on a date with a guy she had just met and liked.

She composed herself and posed the question, "Did you know that nearly every age lays claim to the stones. Some archaeologists believe they are Neolithic, some believe they are early Bronze, some believe middle Bronze and even some believe they are late Bronze but they're way out." Beth dismissed this last group scornfully. "Even the Druids tried to lay claim to the stones but in truth, the Druids arrived in the area about 2,000 years after they had been erected."

Beth took another swallow of the deep red wine. James watched her become more and more excited as she talked about her stones. Her passion was on the surface, there was nothing pretentious about her and she wore her heart on her sleeve. She exuded interesting information, not dreary dates and facts but lurid legends about monks and childless couples. She made the history of the stones exciting. She made the chronological changes from wooden circles of posts and surrounding ditches to the current circle of stones sound like a story unfolding.

When she spoke he could feel her obsession with the stones. It was as if she was brushing against old friends at a party; as if she wanted to introduce him to each of them in turn these weren't stones, these were her friends. She made them come alive. It was as if she was stroking the stones when she spoke, as if she was touching their sleeves, wanting them to whisper their stories to him. She acknowledged them as she walked beneath them in her mind; she looked up at their splendour and was in awe of their spectacle.

James watched her become animated and her eyes told him she had the stones through and through her. Her nose wrinkled up when she talked of some of the spurious, shallow research being conducted and her nostrils flared when she talked of those who wanted to build a bigger visitor centre closer to the stones so the visitors didn't have to walk so far, 'poor lambs'. "The builders dragged and carried the stones 150 miles and the visitors complained of walking 150 yards," she mocked.

James enjoyed being with her. She gave off an energy that was infectious. They talked about circles they had each visited and rated them for views, intrigue and most of all atmospheres. They talked about legends and stories of the stones and the more she drank the more she became excited. She became cross that everybody just accepted the traditional theory of the stones and the link with Midsummer's Day without challenging them, she became angry that there were people who wanted to dig up the stones again and again to examine the artefacts beneath. She declared they had been disturbed too often and was able to prove that, as a result, some of the stones had been replaced in the wrong positions. The more animated she became the more she drank, the more she drank, the more she spilt things and knocked things over. James liked her passion and warmed to her honesty.

Then she furtively looked around the restaurant and pulled her chair to James's side of the table not to be heard by anyone. Slurring her words slightly she whispered, "There's a secret at Stonehenge you know," and she looked around the restaurant again. "The stones hold a secret. I think I've found it. It's all because they re-erected them all wrong. When they put them back up they lined them up to suit Aubery's theories about their origins and the sun. But they got it all wrong." There was a long pause. "I know." She tapped her nose knowingly and then all but passed out. James ordered a room for her and with the aid of the female hotel manager settled her in. He organised a taxi to take her to work in the morning after arranging for her to be woken early with a light breakfast to be served in her room. He paid the bill for everything, deposited money for the taxi on the bedside table and left, leaving a note, thanking her for a lovely evening and promising to get in touch.

James drove back to London deep in thought. A number of things troubled him. The challenge of what he still had to do before the next Midsummer's Day concerned him greatly, and how strange it was that this Beth had come tumbling into his life just at this moment. He smiled when he thought of her tapping her nose knowingly telling him of her secret, eyes half closed.

12

"£1.3m and I'll take it for cash with no chain," James held his hand out to clinch the deal. The vendor of the six en-suite bedroomed, four reception rooms, property in Marlow, Buckinghamshire ignored his hand, walked slowly past him to the window of his lounge and looked out at the 3/4 acre of secluded garden and 25 metre-heated pool. He sighed a resigned vendor's sigh brought about by financial misfortune, turned and, shaking his head sorrowfully said, "Deal." They shook hands, James confirmed his lawyers would be in touch in the morning and he left to return to the City that had made the purchase possible.

Immediately on his return from Wales, James had been summoned into the International Financial Boutique Owners' office and made an offer to become the CEO. He negotiated his package up slightly, as was expected, but the offer was further sweetened by a huge golden handshake that made the Buckinghamshire house purchase immediately possible. He decided to keep his newly acquired promotion and the purchase of the new house from his partner for the present, his partner being his third objective.

James returned to his own office, ordered coffee and water, switched all his phones to silent, had all calls diverted and sat there in silence. For all his money and possessions James was already desperately unhappy. For all his corporate courage and boardroom bravado he now felt very alone. From the moment he had woken back at the Moel Ty Uchaf stone circle his heart had sunk, he knew he'd got it wrong. He'd made a huge mistake. He'd left the most beautiful woman he'd ever met who loved him dearly and he bitterly regretted his decision. He sat there for ages with his head in his hands wondering what he could do. He imagined the scene for the hundredth time. Eira would have woken up to find a sobbing Sion who would be saying through his tears, "James has gone. I saw him go. Why has he gone?"

Sion would be asking, "What did I do wrong to make him leave?" Sion would be inconsolable. Eira would be having the same conversation with herself. What did she do wrong? What else could she have done for him? Did she not love him enough? Did she not excite him any more? Was he not attracted to her any more? What had gone wrong? She would be questioning her very understanding of the word love. James felt so bad.

James had already decided to go back as soon as he could i.e. in one year's time but his black mood reinforced the decision to return, not just as he was, but taking as many things with him to make their combined lives easier. He decided to enhance his medical and healing skills and also return with as much knowledge as he could to help their agrarian society become more productive.

It was six weeks since his visit to Wales and he still found himself deep in thought staring into coffee cups for forgiveness, wondering whatever possessed him to think that his corporate world and shallow friends were more important than what he had just left? He had just swapped a cosy, warm home with a wonderful woman who loved him dearly and beautiful boy who adored him, for a six bedroomed empty house. What the hell did he need six bedrooms for anyway? Like all material things in life, once acquired it soon lost its appeal to him.

His house in Marlow now had a tick beside it.

His CEO's job now had a tick beside it.

The easiest two of the five, post-Wales objectives he'd promised himself before he left the stone circle had already been achieved and he was only in week six of 52. The third objective he acknowledged was going to be trickier; the breaking up of his relationship with his partner. She was a single-minded woman who didn't take prisoners. She had established herself in a man's City world and had blasted through the concrete ceiling early in her career. She was in when he returned home from work early on a Friday and he feared this could turn out to be the fight of the Titans.

He had foresightedly insisted on a pre-nuptial agreement when they first decided to live together on The Royal Crescent, Holland Park in London. They had bought one of the few remaining houses that had not been converted into flats. Both of them had fallen in love with the white stucco painted crescent and its proximity to the actual park and the Kyoto Japanese Gardens. It had been a huge investment for them both. As such James felt sure she would contest every letter in the document. He had paid a fortune for the agreement to be originally drawn up and now was the time for the lawyers to earn their money and protect his assets.

He went into the lounge and poured himself a large whisky.

"Bit early isn't it?"

"Not for the discussion we are about to have."

She didn't understand but decided for James to be home at 5.30pm on a Friday and pouring himself a large whisky, things were going to get serious. She stood up and went over to pour herself a gin and tonic thinking hard as she went. Had he found out about her little 'indiscretions', had he lost his job in the cut-throat world in which he lived where careers were won and lost in a board room meeting, did he required financing to get straight? She decided to wait and see what unfolded.

"It's over between us," said James sitting across the kitchen table from her holding the whisky glass in both hands to warm the amber liquid.

"Has been for some while. I think you know it and I certainly feel it. I want us to split up as amicably as we can."

There was a long silence as the situation sunk in, a situation not entirely unexpected but earlier than she would have liked. They both knew there would never be a right time for this conversation.

"OK we split everything 50/50 and I'll find somewhere else to live," she said quickly.

"No, we work to the letter of the pre-nups and you can take anything you want that's not nailed down."

Another long silence while this high-powered woman thought at 100 mph.

"Cars?"

"Take your pick."

"I'll take the Aston," she tested.

"OK."

She was surprised by his acquiescence. She knew James well and what he wanted he always achieved, this had to be part of a much bigger plan or there was something else he wanted.

"Pictures and furniture?"

"Take what you want."

"James, are you saying you don't want anything of the last, however many years we've been together?"

"Nothing," and with that he put his Aston Martin keys on the table in front of her and went for a shower.

No shouting, no screaming, nothing. He couldn't decide if he was relieved or disappointed but had the good sense to realise that this could well be just round 1.

The shower water was so welcome. It seemed to help wash away a level of guilt he had been wrestling with for six weeks since leaving Eira. He found it difficult to concentrate, he couldn't sleep, he couldn't do anything other than work. He deserved to suffer for what he'd done to that lovely family. He should have stayed. Try as he might he couldn't get Eira out of his head; everywhere he looked he saw her big trusting eyes and soft warm smile. It broke his heart when he thought of Sion and Meg in those last few moments on the mountain. The shower washed away all signs of tears that had started to well up in his self-induced torment. What the hell had he been thinking?

James went for the 100th time to the cupboard where he kept his walking clothes and smelled the sprig of mint sewn into the collar of his cagoule. It was his only reassurance that he hadn't dreamt the whole thing. It was the only tangible thing as a reality check that three thousand years ago had actually happened. Based on that sprig of mint he had already made a

12-month plan to the day and it was well under way. Nothing was going to stop him going back to Eira.

James went into the kitchen to prepare something to eat to be met by his partner putting the concluding ingredients together for a white wine risotto for two. A risotto sprinkled with his favourite cheese, it smelled good, really good. There was a bottle of Pouilly Fuisse complete with its wet, frosty overcoat from the wine chiller already on the table. The table had been laid for two.

James wondered if she was about to seduce him? Probably not. Was she about to try to persuade him not to go? Not in her nature. Was she about to try to soften him into agreeing to the 50/50 split instead of the pre-nups? The most likely option. Was she angry? She didn't seem to be. Perhaps she was just intrigued. He decided to wait and see what developed; ever mindful he was dealing with a formidable adversary.

They sat facing each other. She poured the chilled wine into two balloon glasses. They both raised their glasses at the same time but as neither could think of an appropriate toast they just chinked and he thanked her for cooking. She served slowly and deliberately, occasionally catching his eye to try to read what was happening. There followed a series of slowly posed questions, some out of real interest and others out of her competitiveness not to lose anything of hers to anyone, ever.

"Is she pretty?"

There was a long pause while James deliberately finished what he was eating, and then he looked straight at her.

"Very."

"Welsh?"

Again a long pause as he moved the risotto around the plate.

"Very."

"What's her name?"

"Eira."

"Is she blonde or brunette?"

"Eira means snow in Welsh, apparently the colour of her hair when she was born. She's still very blonde, a natural blonde."

"Eyes?"

"Two," joked James trying to lighten the interrogation.

"I meant what colour?"

"Very blue."

"How old is she?"

"Three thousand years old."

James's partner took a long drink of the chilled white wine, shook her head slowly and said.

"Been going on long?"

"Either 1/2 an hour or a year I really don't know for sure."

"James this is not making any sense."

"Nor to me, nor to me," he repeated and sighed. With that he rose from the table, thanked her for the meal, thanked her for the last, however many years as though it was part of the meal, took a decanter of single malt and a crystal glass from the cupboard and went upstairs to sleep in the guest bedroom.

Late that night he heard his Aston Martin crunching over the short gravel drive followed by its distinctive roar as it drove off into the night.

13

Although James was focussed on his post Moel Ty Uchaf objectives, every so often Beth from the kiosk at Stonehenge slipped back into his thinking. What did she mean, 'there's a secret' and 'they put the stones back up to suit the current thinking not where they were placed originally'. He decided Beth, like him, knew the stones held more, much more. He felt of all the people he knew she was the only one who would understand if he told her of his experiences. But right now he was fully engaged on his own project but when he felt further forward with his objectives he would pick up with her again.

Three out of five post Moel Ty Uchaf objectives had been met, two to go.

James threw himself into work and moved into his Buckinghamshire house. His P.A. presented him with a range of weekend courses to learn to become a paramedic technician as requested, none of which appealed. Somehow, he secured for himself a place with an ambulance team for a period of six months working solely at weekends. His P.A. felt sure the deal had been lubricated by financial inducements.

6.00am every Saturday and Sunday James was walking into the ambulance station and, more often than not, was out on a 'shout' before he had finished his first coffee. He saw every type of road accident and was sent to every type of domestic medical problem. Contrary to the other paramedics James couldn't get enough experience and would opt to go on another shout as soon as he was back. He learned every trick in the book to assist people who were trapped by working closely with the other emergency services. He saw every type of children's ailments and found out how to treat them not only with conventional medicines but also from his other studies, with homeopathic remedies.

Only once in the six months did he get into trouble with his ambulance crew and that was at a stabbing in a particularly unsavoury housing estate. As they were treating an injured man for what turned out to be a messy flesh wound with no vital organs involved, a hail of stones hit the ambulance. Now he had heard of this type of incident caused by youths before but couldn't believe it would actually happen. As they were behind the ambulance the three of them were relatively safe but the whole crazy situation of these good paramedics trying to save a young man's life and being hampered by thugs angered James. He said he wouldn't be long and disappeared into the darkness despite their protestations.

The stones suddenly stopped. And then the paramedics looked up to see a smiling James pushing an old shopping trolley complete with a wonky wheel loaded with two bodies draped over it and one inside. The stab victim had been carefully loaded in the ambulance by the paramedics and James unceremoniously loaded the other three into the back as well. After about six miles on the journey to the hospital James roughly woke the three up and suggested they had a choice. Get out here and make your own way back or stay in the ambulance to meet with the police at the hospital. His phone video footage of the three of them throwing stones at the ambulance helped them decide. They were bundled out in a lay-by near the hospital and James threw their mobiles into the river.

With the stab victim safely in the hands of the A&E team at the hospital, the two paramedics turned, did a high five with James and treated him to cream cakes and coffee.

There was a reason for pushing himself harder and harder with the ambulance crew that kept him so focussed. It was his intention to pass everything he learned onto Eira and to administer more competently to the illnesses and accidents of the village folk. It was his way of atoning for what he had done.

Nine months of the year had already flown by.

14

Professor Brendon Quail was becoming more and more concerned about the lack of information and pushed his third party to keep an even closer watch on Beth. His concern was not so much the lack of progress, but the speed his life was ebbing away. He had lost his wife to his obsession three months ago, his children visited irregularly and then only through guilt and he had mortgaged his house to the maximum to pay for the surveillance team. His funds had initially been extensive but not forever could he afford to pay five sets of secret wages. He was becoming desperate.

There seemed to be an acceleration in the deterioration of his liver and his breathing was becoming erratic. Oxygen pipes tethered him to his desk these days and all the tell-tale symptoms that displayed the inevitable shutdown of his complete system were evident. The deterioration spurred his resolve. An announcement from him about his ground breaking research prior to 'Conference' would be sufficient for him to have achieved his life-long goal. To be around to see any part of a presentation would be a bonus.

He pored over the new diaries; like all the rest they contained all of her movements for the past week. Her propensity to spend long periods of her evenings in the proximity of three particular stones intrigued him. He deduced these must be critical positions and he spent the next week examining every aspect of sight line during the day and the night from his laboratory. His computers laboured trying to articulate the findings but the result was always the same - there was no correlation between the lines of sight and any solar activity. Frustrated, he threw his pen at the wall and put his head in his hands and swayed from side to side. This approach was too slow.

***

James was still intrigued by the conversation he had with Beth and longed to hear more about her 'secret'. He needed to know more about her because she might be the only person in the world he could share his secret Moel Ty Uchaf experience with.

Back in his financial boutique in London, he employed, as did every other financial organisation, a company of investigators. The sums of money he dealt with needed rigorous Due Diligence outside the normal financial, 'in the public domain' stuff. They were good, very, very good. He had decided to get back in contact with Beth and short of going there himself in the hope she was still there, 'his people' could elicit the information far quicker than he ever could.

James's 'people' found out Beth's name and telephone number and address. They confirmed she was who she said she was; a year three, PhD student studying Late Bronze Age history focussing on Stonehenge. They were able to furnish him with all of her bank details, genealogy, medical records and pin numbers if he needed them. They also confirmed she was upsetting the classical academic thinking and her modernist ideas were getting her into some trouble. James's 'people' also reported that she was developing a following of like-minded people who were anxious to be part of her independent research. However, having been ridiculed by many of these originally she was in no particular hurry to share her findings with any of them despite inducements.

James rang despite several months elapsing.

"Hi Beth, it's James, remember me?"

"Of course I do." A long pause followed from Beth's end before she said: "I need to thank you for that evening and well... you know... not taking advantage of me when I got, well... a bit tiddly."

"No problem, forget it. Fancy dinner again tonight?"

There was a pause, a long pause. This wasn't like her at all.

"Not tonight," she replied, but after counting offered, "Wednesday night would be good."

"Wednesday night it is then," but before he could make the arrangements Beth carried on talking quickly. James just listened. She rambled on about their previous conversation about the number of stones in other circles that James had no recollection of, and then finished with, "so that's the reason there are 45 stones at Moel Ty Uchaf."

James twigged that she was either not on her own or being listened to so decided to play along.

"Well, that's solved that little mystery. Let's go to a little pub we talked about last time. I think it's called 'A Yard of Bread'. I'll see you there Wednesday at seven OK?"

"Great, see you then and this time I promise not to get as tiddly."

She hung up.

James looked at the phone for a long time. Beth knew perfectly well there were 41 stones at Moel Ty Uchaf. She had told him last time they met. She'd read the book. She knew it off by heart.

The phrase 'upsetting the classical academic thinking' came to mind from 'his people' so did her words 'the stones hold a secret and I know the secret'.

James made another call to 'his people'.

15

There was just one more objective to achieve and just three months in which to achieve it. James had watched the ineffective bows and arrows being used on the hunting trips by the people of Llandrillo. It had been pitiful to watch. If they did hit anything they did by pure luck and not skill. More often than not, they wounded the poor animal and had to track it for days often losing their quarry in the end. James set himself the task of understanding how to make an effective bow and all the arrows required in the three month period left.

Two months in and he hadn't scratched the surface of the ancient art of bow making. His archer colleagues advised him that there was another easier method and that was to use a crossbow. At first the idea didn't appeal but as the time before Midsummer's Day shortened down to weeks he took up the idea in desperation. In two weeks, with evening and weekend tuition he became proficient enough to hit a playing card at 90 yards. This was the answer he had been looking for. This would make such a difference to their ability to provide good fresh meat in the summer and winter. He bought the best small crossbow that money could buy and 200 bolts.

James dove into the car park of the hotel next door to the 'The Yard of Bread' restaurant with rooms where he was to meet Beth. He was driving his ex's Range Rover, a slightly less ostentatious car than the Aston. He had become caught up in the intrigue. He entered the restaurant from the back door and was met by Beth who gave him an unexpected big hug but under her breath she pleaded, "Please don't say anything in here please, please."

James dutifully sat down and picked up the conversation as if nothing had happened. They talked about his job and the last time they were here and how embarrassed she had been when she woke the next morning. She had been brought her breakfast by the same member of the hotel staff who had helped her to her room the night before. The hotel employee had assured her nothing had happened.

James and Beth ate the meal and both drank just a little wine this time. When they had both finished Beth said, "I've booked in. I hope you don't mind."

"Not at all, I was rather hoping you would."

James paid the bill and the two of them wound their way through the myriad of corridors up to the bedroom. Once inside, she led him into the bathroom and switched on the shower.

"I'm being followed, I know you'll think I'm nuts but now I'm sure of it."

"I know," he said.

Without stopping she continued, "I'll try to explain and then tell me if you believe me. I'm really not paranoid but I'm getting more scared by the day...." There was a long pause when suddenly she quizzically looked at him and said, "What do you mean you know?"

He sat her on the edge of the bath and talked quietly above the noise of the shower: "I believed you the last time when you said you knew the secret of Stonehenge but you weren't making much sense so I did a bit of investigating myself. It turns out that you are upsetting a huge number of people. Some of who are a bit nasty. You have been watched by the five security guards at Stonehenge every day. They record your every move then send their diaries to a PO Box in Maidenhead. If anything happens that can't wait, they phone a special number and leave a report. The messaging system is based in Paris."

Beth looked at him open mouthed.

"This can't be happening to me?"

"It is. It all traces back to a Professor Brendon Quail in Oxford. It transpires he is behind the whole thing and it's he who is paying the security guards to report on you. Do you know him?"

"The bastard," she spat the words. "When I was an undergraduate he tried to seduce me in return for a higher grade. I punched him in the mouth, not my finest hour but my most satisfying. My personal tutor took up my case and it all got hushed up. I got a First 'cos I deserved it. Then Quail became interested again when I did my Masters as I was doing some fancy theory bashing stuff which was upsetting some people. He wanted me to write a paper on my findings and he would co-edit it. I refused. He would have taken all the glory. So it looks as if he intends to steal my findings anyway, the bastard. And you say the five guards have been spying on me all this time?"

"James we have to go to Stonehenge tonight. That's why, when you rang the other day, it wasn't the right day. I'll share the secret with you. Stonehenge was never built around the solar solstice; it was built around the lunar cycles. Tonight is a special night and I need someone with me who I trust. I need someone to distract the security guard. Will you come? I quite understand if you don't want to get involved but now I know you a bit better I would really like you to help me."

"I'm not doing anything else tonight so let's go and bust the Stonehenge secret wide open," said James, caught up in her enthusiasm.

They parked and walked the last mile to Stonehenge. As planned, Beth made her way to the stones across the road and James broke into the Stonehenge bookshop on site as quietly as possible and set it alight. James watched as the flames grew and their reflection interfered with the TV screen in the security cabin. The security guard tumbled out of his office and ran to see if he could do anything. When he realised there was nothing he could do on his own he ran back to the office and rang the fire brigade. Once

James was sure the security guard was fully engaged with the blaze he headed off to join Beth at the stones through the mist. He found Beth trying to line up two stones that wouldn't line up. She was using string across the circle. When James arrived she made him hold the ball of string and then moved sideways one step, then another.

"Tell me what you're doing," pleaded James.

"Many, many years ago those two stones fell down and it was agreed to re-erect them in the early 1900s. They did all sorts of surveys and decided that they were slightly out of place to allow the sun to come through on the summer solstice. To let the sun through they moved them about eighteen inches to the right, a perfect line of sight for the sun on one day of the year, the summer solstice. Only the stones weren't put up for the sun they were put up for the moon. Tonight is one of the nights in the year when you should be able to see the line of sight of the moon and whatever is the secret of the stones. As I can't move the stones I have calculated that if you move three paces to the right and move slightly into the centre of the circle, you won't get anything like the full effect, but you will be able to see something."

Their discussions were interrupted by the sirens of the fire brigade.

Beth moved to her pre-determined position. The skies cleared, the moon appeared, the mists started to clear when James heard the security guard shout, he was about a hundred yards away. James said to

Beth, "Do what you have to do and use only this phone if you need to contact me," and he pushed a small, yellow mobile phone into her jeans pocket. She smiled and kissed his cheek.

"Thanks."

James turned and ran off diagonally followed by the security guard. James allowed the guard to think he could catch him by running at a slightly slower pace than the guard. When they were about half a mile away from the circle James sprinted off into the darkness leaving the guard panting helplessly on the grass.

In the silent circle the moonbeam shone across the stones and just a knife-edge of light settled on Beth's head, the rest obscured by the wrongly re-erected stones. She walked towards the beam. James looked back but lost sight of her in the mist.

16

Back in his house in Marlow James arranged all the things he wanted to take on his return to Llandrillo in one room - medicines, books on old remedies, tools, knives and the cross bow and bolts. With all that came the things he wanted to take as presents for Eira, Sion, Nain and Taid. He even managed to secrete some sweets into the load for the children and some big fireworks for a party.

Loading everything into the rucksack accounted for only half of what he wanted to take. So a repacking exercise despatched all the medicines to a strong holdall and the tools to the rucksack. The crossbow was strapped outside. He could barely lift the rucksack, just like being back in the army he thought to himself. Just two days to go.

James drove the Land Rover to Llandrillo and stayed in Room 1 at Tyddyn Llan for an extra day. It transpired that the Land Rover was a much more suitable vehicle than the Aston Martin for what he had in mind.On the morning of the midsummer solstice he wished himself a happy birthday, enjoyed a leisurely full Welsh breakfast and drove as near to the site of the circle as he could and parked. First he carried the rucksack up to the stone circle followed by a second journey for the holdall. The time was 11.00am. the sun was nearly as high as it could get, the sky was clear and James was as excited as a child. He imagined himself walking down the village track and being surrounded by children all cheering, each one receiving a long lasting lolly or its equivalent.

He visualised Sion coming out to see what all the noise was about and then running to meet him. He could see, in his mind's eye, Nain and Taid standing together at the doorway of their house surrounded by tiny children smiling and gesturing him to go into Eira's house. But most of all he wanted to hold Eira. He wanted to hold her so tight and tell her he loved her and was sorry for all the hurt he had caused. He ached for that first hug, for the first kiss. He so wanted her to accept him back.

At 11.59am he slid down the biggest stone facing inwards wearing his rucksack and pulled the holdall into himself. He whistled Meg and she came immediately. James closed his eyes and despite his excitement quickly fell into a deep, deep sleep.

He woke and looked around the site. He was as nervous as a kitten that it was the right era. Could the gods have conspired against him? They had offered him one chance to be happy and he had, albeit, thrown it away. They could have delivered him into another less glamorous time where plagues and war ravaged the land. From where he sat he could see he was certainly in another time, for the stones were the taller and forests were everywhere. However, it wasn't until he stood up did he discover in the middle of the circle the blackened stones from Barnaby's funeral pyre. He gave such a sigh of relief. After looking around to make doubly sure everything was as he had left it three thousand years ago, he started off down the Old Drover's Road with his heavy load.

Thinking of his reception he just couldn't get there fast enough, so decided to leave the holdall about half way down to the village as the weight was cutting into his hands. He hid it near one of the streams that crossed the track and carried on with just the rucksack.

It was when he returned to the track after depositing the holdall he heard a scream, a scream that made all the hairs on his neck stand up. He moved back off the track and into the tree line to find a vantage point from where he could see who or what had uttered the scream. Every nerve in his body throbbed, adrenaline raced around every muscle and back to his heart. Something was wrong, very wrong. Hidden behind two big oak trees, about one hundred yards from the centre of the village, he could see that the thatched roof of one of the houses on the far side of the village was on fire.

Then he spotted, outside the house nearest to him, about 50 yards away, two big armed men in ragged fur skins in the courtyard of the house. One man was about 6ft and the other was shorter but stockier. Each had a crude bow across their back and a quiver full of arrows. One warrior held a club and the other a spear with a flinthead. Both men were heavily tattooed. Their matted hair hung in twisted straggles down their faces and down their backs. The Hunllef, thought James and a place deep in his stomach churned remembering the stories Eira had told him of rape and murder.

He remembered they took the young and healthy for slaves and the children for, God only knew what reason. His thoughts were for Eira and Sion. The two warriors were ugly, they were menacing and they were aptly named, The Day Nightmare People, the Hunllef. Their language was guttural and deep coming out in short bursts like exploding air. Their movements were slow and cumbersome as though their huge frames were too big for their legs. They seemed bent on damage, any kind of damage. They kicked over the small benches outside the house; they kicked over the little water butt and ripped down the fences that enclosed the chickens. Chickens that came close to them were necked and tossed aside. Senseless destruction designed to intimidate.

James watched the bigger man, who was holding an old woman, shake her like a doll. Her silver hair spread backwards and forwards across her face. From her mouth came a choking, gargling sound as she struggled for breath. James recognised her as the old lady who had looked after Sion when the village folk had arranged his surprise party. She was a gentle old lady who couldn't harm anyone. Then suddenly, out from the little house came her husband brandishing an oak root club. Screaming, he ran straight for the big Hunllef who was holding his wife.

As he ran his bowed, spindly legs showed as his robes parted in the front; he was an old, old man. James couldn't help but feel a sense of admiration for the old man as he covered the courtyard fearlessly towards the Hunllef. But before the old man reached his target a club wielded by the smaller Hunllef caved in the back of his head and he fell to the floor, a limp, crumpled, lifeless form.

Thick, black/red blood from his wound immediately made a pool in the dirt around his head. James felt sick; the whole incident was over in a second. Neither of the two Hunllef gave him a second glance. Then the struggling old woman turned and saw her husband lying there in a pool of his own blood. She lashed out with a fury only known to women.

The bigger Hunllef threw the old woman to the floor and raised his spear in both hands above his head. She didn't care, she had one objective and that was to crawl to be with her husband, whatever the cost. James had taken the rucksack off, freed the crossbow and located a bolt in a second. He sighted the big Hunllef and fired, imagining there to be a playing card attached to his chest. Before the big Hunllef's spear had started its decent a hole appeared in the warrior's chest, a hole big enough to insert a man's index finger. The exit hole was much bigger. The bolt had collected part of the Hunllef's sternum along with pieces of shattered ribs from the chest and tore a hole out of his back the size of a dinner plate taking organs, ribs and sternum with it. Having been lifted off the ground with the impact of the bolt he was thrown backwards about six feet. The Hunllef's heart pumped blood into the void where his aorta had been until there was no more blood left, only froth and his body shuddered into death.

The frightened, shorter Hunllef immediately grabbed his bow and loaded an arrow. Crouching, he looked all around. James's next crossbow bolt was in place and had the second Hunllef's name on it if he touched the old woman.

James suddenly remembered the old man who had been murdered so casually was the very same old man who had taught him how to set up and use a woodland lathe. He'd been so patient with James and they had laughed together at James's clumsiness. Now he was dead, a senseless death leaving a widow in this harsh world to survive on her own. The old woman crawled to her knees behind the wary Hunllef and came across her dead husband's oak root club in the dirt. In a semi-conscious state she lifted the club, rose to her feet and sprang from behind at the second Hunllef giving him a glancing blow to the side of his head. He turned in a rage and swung his bow at her knocking her sideways. Still in a rage he turned his back on his unseen enemy like all thugs, to take his anger out on the weak. The Hunllef wiped the trickle of blood caused by the blow to his forehead with his fore arm, raised his bow as she lay there on the dirt floor and took aim at the unconscious, crumpled form of the old woman. The Hunllef's arrow had not even been brought to half way back on his bow when James's second bolt found its mark.

This time the bolt passed through his back and out of his chest leaving an exit hole the same size as the entry hole. The Hunllef spun around and around by the force of the bolt. He crashed through a wicker pen and flopped in a contorted heap in the dirt unable to understand what had hit him. He tried in vain to stem the flow of blood from his chest with his hand, but within a minute of spluttering and coughing blood out of his mouth the gaping hole in his chest had beaten him and his eyes finally closed never to harm another soul.

James ran down to the scene of carnage only to be confronted by the old woman on her knees preparing to defend herself against him. James shushed her gently not to raise the alarm and bring more Hunllef down on them and moved closer for her to recognise him. When her misty eyes recognised him her spirit gave way and she crumpled to the ground. James squeezed some water into her dry mouth, held her head and stroked her hair till she came around.

"What did they want?" James whispered.

Through a series of wracking sobs she said, "They wanted us to tell them where the village children had gone but we wouldn't tell them so they killed my husband."

"How many of them are there?"

"Many."

James looked around. He needed to get right into the centre of the village without the Hunllef knowing, if he was to have any element of surprise. Then he remembered the tunnel he had created with the village men that led from the centre of the village out to the tree line. They had excavated the tunnel so the children could get out of the village without being seen if there had been no warning about the Hunllef. He said a little prayer that the children had managed to flee in time. He decided to use the tunnel in reverse.

James left the old woman sobbing, cradling the head of her dead husband in her lap; it was a pitiful sight and James swore someone would pay. He made his way to the tunnel exit. All the timbers were off where the children had escaped inside the tree line. They would now all be safely inside the cave near Sedd y Cawr, the giant's seat. If all had gone according to plan the older ones would have helped the little ones and now they should be as safe as they ever could be in the underground cave.

James dropped down into the little tunnel and quietly crawled along moving his crossbow in front of him. The tunnel had only been excavated for the children so several times he had to lie flat out to make progress over roots and stones. Eventually, he arrived at the entrance of the tunnel in the centre of the village hidden inside Nain and Taid's house. He climbed out and covered the entrance back over so that the casual observer wouldn't notice. Peering out through the wicker window he could see there were about 20 of the Hunllef outside Nain and Taid's house. A long line of young village boys and men were tied with a rope around their necks and a further rope was tied to their right ankle so they would have to walk in sync. James's heart sank when he saw Sion at third in line. He retreated back inside the house to think.

A scream accelerated his thinking. He recognised it as having come from Nain. She was being held by a rat-faced Hunllef. Her face was bloodied and her dress was torn and splashed with blood. James loaded a bolt, stood up and walked boldly out into the area in front of the house. There was a sudden silence as the Hunllef saw him. They all took a few steps back forming a semi-circle around the lonely James. A strange man in strange clothes appearing from nowhere required some caution.

James summoned up all his courage and spoke to the assembled group in the strongest tone he could muster.

"Let her go. What band of warriors are you to wage war on old women?"

There was consternation as the Hunllef turned to their leader for guidance.

The obvious leader stood warily watching and listening to James. All the time he nervously changed his upright spear from hand to hand. He was a huge, bald, hunch-backed man dripping with the trinkets and trophies of war. Pieces of skulls and feathers adorned his huge frame. They hung from around his neck; they hung from his wrists and ankles. A fur tabard was covered in the filth of spilled food and drink and the matted fur and his filthy body stank in the hot sun. His body was covered in scars and tattoos; tattoos that originally had been swirls and stars no longer clearly delineated but smudged and weathered on the old skin canvas like spilled ink. The blackened and broken teeth from tearing meat off the bones and fighting made him an awesome sight. Saliva dribbled from one side of his mouth as he panted in the hot sun.

His enormous head moved slowly from side to side as his bloodshot, pig eyes squinted to focus. He was weighing up this new quarry. James and he were facing each other about 30 yards apart.

"Take your men and leave."

"Never return to this village."

"You have angered the gods."

"Leave or the gods of thunder and fire will descend on you and your kin."

James was conscious that communicating with this warrior was all but impossible so with every sentence he also reinforced the message by hand gestures.

One man against 20, James was normally comfortable in his own skin but here he felt very vulnerable, very alone. These were regular killers with no compunction; they would kill just to demonstrate their prowess. He had no idea how long his bravado would ensure the Hunllef kept their distance. His only hope was that his speed of thinking and his crossbow would keep them at bay.

Suddenly James felt something brush his shoulder. He'd been so focussed on the 20 men in front of him he hadn't noticed one of the village men come and stand beside him. This big, brave man, who had just arrived back in the village from the fields, had missed everything. He saw that here was James, one man, defending his village against 20 Hunllef. The villager held his hunting bow in the non-aggressive downward pose loaded, ready. Then James felt another villager back from trapping rabbits stand on his other side holding his hunting spear. Slowly the group behind him grew to about 20 all carrying weapons; even Taid joined with a club. These men behind James weren't fighters, they were hunter-gatherers in the main and if it did kick off James knew there'd be carnage, but this was such a show of spirit from the villagers. Finally, they were joined by some of the women folk holding sticks and pitchforks and anything they could fight with. There were now about 30 villagers against 20 fighting giants.

There was a stand-off. The leader had watched unconcernedly the numbers swell behind James, ignoring them until they completely tipped the balance. Now he was edgy, now he was twitching not knowing what to do. His men could dispatch these people but there would be a cost to his warriors. And he wasn't sure of the capability of this stranger who had the courage to confront a band of twenty warriors. Someone was going to make the first move.

It came in the form of the rat-faced Hunllef who had been holding Nain. He cast her aside and started to move towards his bow and quiver shouting and gesturing that he wasn't afraid to take on the stranger. He gestured how brave he was, he mimicked his leader for being a woman. He was easy to understand but he was dangerous with his captive audience. He shouted at James to let the gods send fire and thunder; he was ready for them. Rat-Face taunted his leader about his lack of courage and he would show him and all the other warriors that he should be the new leader.

"Tell him to stand still," shouted James at the leader, pointing at Rat-Face. There was no response. Rat-Face continued to defiantly load his bow calling the rest of his band cowards. Calling the leader a coward.

"Tell him to put his bow down now," shouted James at the leader.

No response from the leader just piercing, pig eyes watching, waiting. This was James's trial. The next seconds would determine whether there was an almighty battle or the start of the Hunllef capitulating and retreating. James stepped away from the villagers not wanting anyone to get hurt by an arrow meant for him. With much bow waving, swaggering, theatre and guttural shouting at both the leader and the band of warriors, to demonstrate his bravery Rat-Face slowly levelled his bow at James. At the same time, in one movement, James raised his crossbow and fired at the man's chest. Just as the first bolt had done up at the old couple's house, the bolt entered

143

Rat-Face's chest with a hole the size of an index finger and exited with a hole the size of a man's spread out hand. Rat-Face's blood, organs and ribs were splashed over every warrior behind for 10 yards. At only 25 yards this bolt had continued straight through Rat-Face and on into the stomach of the warrior standing immediately behind him. This second, blood splattered warrior crashed backwards into a tree holding his stomach. Only the bolt flights were visible through his fingers.

James reloaded the crossbow quickly as the Hunllef were distracted examining the ghastly wounds of the two men. He turned to the villagers and told then not to move, yet. Imperceptibly, James edged his way over to a smouldering cooking fire and pushed two Roman candles into the embers. Satisfied they were alight, he watched the blue papers start to fizz. He leaned the loaded crossbow against his leg and held the two Roman candles, one in each hand.

He faced the leader again.

"Take your men and never come to this village again,." he said.

"You have angered the gods and they will rain fire and thunder down upon you."

The leader was watching James warily and deftly spun his spear into the throwing position. His men saw his move and started to bang their spears on the ground in unison. The effect of the deep, low drumming noise on the stone dry earth was terrifying.

The Hunllef started to move forward. The villagers were beginning to nervously move back a step but James was used to the intimidation of noise and shouting in boardrooms and war zones and took no notice. James cursed the long fuse designed to allow people sufficient time to retire safely. He had no idea which Roman candle would fire first so he kept both trained on the leader.

The leader took a step back ready to throw his spear just as the first blast from one of the Roman candles flew out. The swirling fireball of burning magnesium was on target and wound itself into his fur tabard at his stomach level. Almost instantaneously the leader's screams pierced the air as the burning ball of fire, sparks and magnesium melted his skin, muscle and stomach. The loudest of explosions inside the cavity followed. The second Roman candle released its fireball screaming as it targeted another warrior who fell, wrestling with the fire until it found his skin and the white-hot magnesium seared into his body. Then the two Roman candles rhythmically fired screaming balls of fire. Explosion after explosion followed. The noise was deafening, one after another they flew at the Hunllef who were now scrabbling all over each other to put distance between them and this stranger who could throw fire and thunder.

Two of them tried to drag the dying leader away to the sounds of James's voice ringing above the screams of the Hunllef and the explosions.

"Never, ever come here to Llandrillo again."

"Tell your children of the wrath of the gods today."

"Tell your children's children of today."

"Tell all the other tribes of this place and what happens to warriors who come here to make war on these people."

"Never cross this river or cross these mountains again."

The two Roman candles were now spent but there wasn't a sign of the Hunllef. James let the villagers go after them and some of the men dispatched the nearly dead Hunllef, including the leader. The rest accompanied James and followed the Hunllef to the river where they were bathing their burns in the cool water. James let off two more Roman candles aiming as closely as he could to scare rather than maim. Screaming in fear and pain the Hunllef splashed and waded across the river continuing until out of sight and into the forest.

Then all was quiet.

For the first time since he had arrived in the ancient village of LLandrillo James allowed himself to come down from high fight mode to a lower level of preparedness. His breathing slowed down to normal. His heart rate slowed down from overdrive to normal and he allowed himself a moment's peace. He thought back on the whole incident and offered a small prayer acknowledging how badly it could have gone. Now in a calmer frame of mind, on his way back to the village, James reflected that some of his, behind enemy lines action, and City corporate boardroom battles had been a bit hairy with very high life and financial stakes but this really had topped them all.

Back at the village the ropes were being cut from the line of slaves and a clean-up operation was already underway. Several of the villagers were trying to put out the fire in the thatch on the far side of the village. James hurried over to see Nain who was drifting in and out of consciousness. Taid kept thanking and thanking him for what he had done. After examining Nain he reassured Taid that Nain would by O.K. with plenty of rest. James turned to the able-bodied men and women, acknowledged their support and suggested they burn the bodies of the Hunllef well out of the village before the children saw them. He then sent the women to collect the terrified children from up at Sedd y Cawr. As soon as they heard, two of the older women went to take care of the wife of the old woodturner on the edge of the village.

Next, James went looking for Sion.

He heard the boy call his name and turned to see him running towards him but just as they hugged the boy collapsed in his arms exhausted from his ordeal. James carried his limp body home, lay him on his bed, found someone to care for him and then went in search of Eira; the reason he was here in the first place.

His heart was in his mouth. She was the prettiest woman in the village. Her long fair hair would have been a magnet to them; she would have been the first for their pleasure. The thought of the filthy leader touching her pure body was more than he could bear and made him run the faster in search of her or her body. James scoured the village looking, but nobody had seen her. He didn't know whether this was good news or bad. In one of their quiet moments he recalled she had told him that when the Hunllef had finished with a woman they passed her down to lower warriors in the tribe, but some would just kill her so that no other warrior could claim her. His mouth was dry and his stomach was churning. He felt sick. He dreaded turning every corner and coming across her limp, used body.

In one positive moment he wondered if she had taken the children up to Sedd y Cawr but when they returned he was told she hadn't been with the children. His only conclusion was that a group of slaves must have been taken earlier. He decided this was the only explanation and set off for Eira's house to collect some things and go after the Hunllef and bring her back whatever the cost. He estimated there were about eight wounded Hunllef and about six able-bodied warriors left in the band. However, they were leaderless and a rabble. If they had harmed her he didn't know what he would do, from an all out killing spree to just walking away with her body, devastated. He struggled to think coherently.

It was getting dark when he returned to Eira's house to check on Sion who was just coming to. He hugged and hugged the groggy boy. As soon as Sion could speak James asked,

"Where's your mother?"

"She went looking for you," said the boy.

"Me? What do you mean she went to look for me? When?"

"This morning before the Hunllef arrived she decided that today, the summer solstice, was the day she was going to find you. She tied some things up in her shawl, said goodbye to me and went up to the stone circle to dream and follow you. She's missed you so much."

"And I've missed you all so much," his guilt returned and James buried his head next to Sion's on the pillow as the enormity of what Sion had told him, sank in.

James's heart sank. The thought of Eira looking for him in the year of 2000 AD filled him with dread. He looked at his watch. It was still only 11.20 pm on the day of the summer solstice; he still had time.

If he couldn't get back she would have to fend for herself for a whole year in a strange time, maybe forever; it didn't bear thinking about. James had things he had to do before he left. First, he hid the crossbow and bolts in Eira's house and then gave Sion his present, the big sheath knife he'd been carrying since his first encounter with the Hunllef, just in case it got close up and personal with them. Sion's mouth dropped open and his eyes were as wide as saucers when he saw it.

James then went to see Taid who was tenderly nursing Nain and quietly telling her what had happened after she became unconscious. James told Taid where he'd left all of the medicines and his rucksack and asked him if he would arrange for them to be brought to Eira's house and kept dry until he came back with Eira, which he promised faithfully he would do. James hugged him and thanked him for standing with him against the Hunllef; he then hugged Nain and managed to get a weak smile out of her. He promised them again he'd come back and left the village at a run. 30 minutes to get to the stone circle was tight. He collected a patient, tied up, Meg on the way. There was no need to try to sleep, he was exhausted when he slid down the stone at 11.55 pm and as soon as he closed his eyes he was away.

17

James woke, checked around to ensure he was in 2000 AD, noted the time, 12.30 pm and ran to the Range Rover. As he made his slow, bouncy descent down the Old Drover's Road he tried to work out how long Eira could have been here on her own and what she would have done.

He calculated that she had probably been in the year 2000 AD for between two and four hours and thinking the village would be the same, she would have made straight for it to ask around for him. He gunned the Range Rover over a particularly rutted part of the road and cursed every farm gate for slowing him down. He felt so responsible for her; she was so vulnerable.

Eventually, he brought the vehicle to an abrupt stop outside the Dudley Arms in the centre of Llandrillo village and jumped out. A few folk were milling about outside enjoying a drink in the mid-day summer sunshine. They were all clasping their pint glasses in the traditional, cuddle hold; fingers through the handle, hand wrapped around the glass all held lovingly against the chest. James approached them.

"Anyone seen a blonde woman in a faded dress, a bit of a hippy type?"

They all laughed, "One that's frightened of tractors?" asked a local.

"Probably."

"She was asking if we knew of a man called James and where was the house he lived in," said one of the girls as she extinguished her cigarette in a trough of flowers outside the pub."

The girl continued, "She spoke with a strange accent we could hardly understand. Well, we know there's no one in the village called James 'cos most of us have lived here all our lives, but we were having a think about folk who live nearby when a tractor and fully loaded muck trailer came past. She freaked out with the noise as though she'd never seen one before and ran off out of the village."

"Which way?"

They pointed back the way he had just come over the bridge. James shouted thanks and jumped back into the car but decided to stop to think. He could be chasing shadows for days. She could be anywhere. She couldn't have gone far but the longer she was lost the harder she would be to find. Where would she feel safe? Everything was different now, nowhere was the same. The houses were in different places, the river was much bigger than she would have expected and the forests were all gone. Roads and pavements replaced the muddy tracks, cars replaced the rumbling carts and a telephone box, a shop and telegraph poles would have totally confused her. Where would she feel safe? The only place that wouldn't have changed in 3000 years was Sedd y Cawr, the giant's seat and the cave behind it. He started the engine and headed back up the Old Drover's Road again.

The giant's seat was on a track, way off the Old Drover's Road, further up the mountain. Fortunately, he was able to drive all the way. He pulled up next to the huge, weather carved stone in the shape of a seat. He had sat here so many times before with her watching the sun set on the mountain on the other side of the valley. His heart was in his mouth. Where would he go next if she wasn't here? Be positive, be positive he kept telling himself. He jumped out of the vehicle and started towards the stone. If she wasn't here next he would go to the cave. He called softly.

"Eira, it's me, James."

He heard a rustle from behind the stone.

"James?" she moved nervously around the stone so she could see him.

"Yes it's me," he said, holding his arms out to her. James had waited so long for this moment. Never again was he going to let her out of his sight.

She was standing behind the great stone seat holding a bundle of possessions. She was more beautiful than ever he remembered. She stood there as a woman, a strong willed, elegant young woman, her eyes shining with the vibrancy of youth and energy. Her hair was shining in the sunshine moving slightly in the light breeze up there on the mountain. His chest was thumping with the anxiety of not being able to find her and now that he had found her were her feelings the same as his? To him she was just beautiful; nothing had changed except the loneliness of having been away from her for so long.

It was a woman who was looking at him with eyes full of feeling, but it was the bright-eyed girl inside her that threw her possessions to one side and ran to him and hugged him.

There was nothing in the whole wide world he needed more than to be held by Eira. He thought he'd lost her for ever several times that day with the incident with the Hunllef. He knew he would never have recovered had she been violated by one of them. He also knew when he couldn't find her and thought she had been taken that he was about to go after them until every one was dead and she was back with him. He had to banish all these horrible thoughts from his head. Everything was O.K. now. Eira was here, she was safe in his arms and she was his.

She smelled fresh and pure, she felt soft and she needed to be held as much as he did. They couldn't hold each other tightly enough. They embraced and kept moving to hold each other differently as though they were checking they had found the right person. There was no doubt. He had found his lost soul mate and she had travelled across time to find him.

Her feet made their familiar way up onto his walking boots to make her the higher, enabling their faces to move closer and closer until they touched. When their cheeks did touch their breathing changed. The relief in being together again changed into a kiss; the kiss of, I've missed you. The kiss of, I've missed you transformed into an urgent kiss and that urgent kiss tuned into a passion they had both yearned for every waking moment for a year. Three thousand years were wiped away in a second, she had forgiven him and he no longer burned inside with the guilt of leaving.

Their passion raged to be closer and closer and there on the giant's seat, on Mid-summer Day, under an iridescent blue sky they made love in a way neither would ever forget; a way they had both dreamt it would be, every lonely night for a year to this very day. The Berwyn Mountains joined hands and surrounded their immodesty like a curtain and for a while they were invisible to everyone in this world and the last.

They stayed there, not letting go of each other in their own cocoon, talking, laughing and relaying every detail of each other's year as they had done when they lived together and had only been away for a day. This time they'd been apart for what seemed like a life time and both wanted to know about everything.

He told her of his time in her village today and how the Hunllef had hurt people. He told her how he had killed several and persuaded the rest to leave, never to return. He lied about Nain being O.K. but he believed, with rest, she would be and he left out the bits about Sion having been tied in a line of slaves, believing the thought would be too harrowing. Sitting there together on a car rug they looked down on the village she had left three thousand years before and he had left this morning and they slid into a happy silence, giving each other gentle squeezes of reassurance, smiles and confirmation that it was real when there was nothing else to say.

Occasionally, she asked questions about things in this alien age to her. Like the new electricity generating wind turbines on the mountaintops on the other side of the valley. James explained as best he could.

"I don't like wind turbines. I prefer trees."

"So do I."

"What frightened you in the village?"

She pointed at his car.

"One of those only bigger and with a horrible smell."

James laughed at her description, so she playfully pushed him off the stone seat saying,

"It wasn't funny," which made him laugh all the more.

The time was now nearly 3.30 pm and Bala, the only place with any shops for 20 miles, closed at 5pm.

"We need to get you some new clothes. Let's go and see what we can find in Bala."

"Why, what's the matter with what I'm wearing."

"Let's just see, shall we?" suggested James.

He opened the car door and encouraged Eira to get in. He started the engine and she was terrified. Holding onto his arm she cried,

"Make it stop, make it stop."

James reassured her and gently eased the car forward. He tried to understand how it must feel to someone who had never travelled faster than on the old priest, Barnaby's horse and cart, to now be bouncing along on the Old Drover's Road in a top of the range, Range Rover. Slowly but surely she relaxed and started to enjoy the ride in her enormous seat with armrests, she felt like a princess on a throne.

As they entered Llandrillo she asked him to slow down as she strained to recognise anything or anybody in her village. Apart from the old stone bridge she shook her confused head explaining that there were houses but they were all in the wrong places, now they were all different. Her house had been replaced by a modern, half stone and half brick house with a slate roof called Honeysuckle Cottage. She liked the flowers growing over the porch and the small window boxes but it was as if she was in a different village to the one she knew. She asked who lived in the house with the high pointed roof only to be told by James that it was the house where all of the villagers went to worship their God. She wanted to know who lived in the tiny red house that everyone could see into? How do you explain a telephone box to somebody from the late Neolithic period? Thought James. Llandrillo was no longer her village, it was a new village and she dismayed that she recognised so little.

On the way to Bala she started to become more comfortable in the car and asked to go faster and faster like an excited little girl. Several times he found himself reaching over and touching her arm to make sure she was real. Several times he caught her out of the corner of his eye smiling at him. They were both checking it wasn't a dream.

He parked on Bala High Street by the White Lion pub and together they made their way next door to the shop that sold women's clothes. The assistant eyed Eira suspiciously with her bare feet and hippy dress but when she realised Eira was with James she relaxed and became more curious than alarmed.

"Would you please help us to choose some walking trousers and shirts and socks for Eira. Oh, and some walking trainers please?" he asked.

The assistant dutifully led Eira into a cubical and presented her with some Rowan trousers to try on. Ten seconds later a red-faced assistant came from behind the curtains and embarrassedly declared to James, "Sir, are you aware the lady has no underwear?"

"Sorry, I forgot, some underwear as well please. She's been living in a commune up on the Berwyn Mountains for some time. I don't suppose they have much need for underwear up there," was James's lame excuse.

While Eira tried on the new clothes the other assistant asked if they were staying locally, to be told by James that they had one night booked at the hotel called Tyddyn Llan in Llandrillo. The assistant nodded, explained she knew it well and suggested to James that Rowans and Nike walking boots would certainly not be suitable at Tyddyn Llan for the lady for dinner. James hadn't thought further than trousers and a shirt.

30 minutes later and Eira was sporting a new pair of Rowans, a light check shirt, some trainers and a walking jacket. James also noticed her breasts under the check shirt were in a slightly different place too. A further bag was placed on the counter by the first shop assistant of toiletries and 'other essentials' and then a further, larger bag was added by the second assistant who suggested the enclosed would be suitable for the evening and a night at Tyddyn Llan.

James thanked them both for their patience, paid and left loaded with the bags.

He opened the door to Room 1 at Tyddyn Llan and allowed Eira to go in first. She entered slowly trying to take everything in all at once. Walking across to the window Eira ran her long slender fingers down the heavy brocade curtains and across the elaborate tie-backs, comparing the texture with that of the fine net curtains. She touched the wooden backed writing chair and inlaid leather writing desk as she made her way to the antique, four poster bed where she hugged one of the posts, looked at him and said,

"James it's all beautiful."

In checking the softness of the bed and plumped up pillows her hand left indentations on the Egyptian cotton duvet, so immediately she smoothed it all back to perfect as if she was a naughty girl. She traced her fingers around the gold, embossed inlay at the foot of the bed and looked up at the canopy. Her eyes were full of wonderment. He held her hand and led her into the bathroom. He turned on the taps into the cream, high backed bath and the noise made her jump. Eira let the warm water run over her hands and looked wide-eyed behind the taps to see where the water was coming from. He made her smell the soaps and shampoos and once smelled she wouldn't let go of them.

James decided an explanation of the toilet could wait for later.

Eira went across to the window in the bathroom and looked into the garden. She placed both her hands on the cold glass expecting them to go straight through as if nothing was there. She stopped suddenly looked at him and said,

"James, the sunshine and its warmth can come through and we can see out but neither the wind nor the rain can come in, is that right?"

"Exactly," replied James, having the concept of glass explained to him for the very first time, something he had always taken for granted.

Eira was most taken with the electric light switch, which in her eyes, lit all of the candles in the room in one go and then was equally astonished when she switched it off and they were extinguished in one go. Throughout his preparations for dinner James found himself suddenly sitting in the dark as Eira tried the switch, just one more time, and giggled when she turned all the candles back on again.

She eventually came out of the bathroom wearing the clothes the second shop assistant had selected for her. James could only stand up, put his glass of single malt down and stare at the apparition. She was beautiful. Eira had washed her hair and combed it till it shone gold. A sleeveless, silver top fitted her perfectly and a tasteful 'v' accentuated her sculptured cleavage. There was no need for adornments or paint or powder, it would be impossible to improve on perfection. A long black linen skirt exaggerated her work-honed, athlete's figure and a pair of lightweight, black court sandals with a tiny heel finished off the whole outfit.

The second shop assistant had demonstrated her knowledge of her craft very well. Over her shoulders, Eira wore a pale cream cashmere stole, the ends threaded between her arms and her body. She was stunning and she loved him and she was here in the year 2000. There was nothing else he could possibly want.

He led her down the creaking, highly polished stairs with its wobbly banister, through the bar with its display of thimbles on the wall and high-backed antique chairs in every corner and into the restaurant. The restaurant was furnished with antique furniture and drapes, all complemented by ornaments chosen tastefully by the owner's eccentricity. Eira, in her new outfit had become taller, more elegant and most importantly, happy. A happiness that glowed from within. She walked slowly with dignity, poise and the carriage of a lady, comfortable in these new surroundings. Heads turned as together they wound their way between the occupied, white linen covered tables. Tables covered in forests of glasses. Conversations ended abruptly, wine glasses stopped on the way to lips, forkfuls of food hung motionless in the air on their upward journey and plump wives tried to regain the attention of their bored husbands.

Whispers from tables of regulars explaining to friends that, 'he normally sits on his own and reads a book over dinner,' and, 'we've never seen him here with anyone before,' and, 'she really is quite beautiful' drifted across the restaurant. They were shown to a table in the small alcove that had a view out onto the illuminated lawn where solar lanterns lined the gravel drive. Eira's eyes were everywhere hoping not to embarrass him in any way. James moved her seat back to make it easier for her to sit down and when seated, removed her stole and placed it on the back of her chair. He put his hands on her shoulders, kissed her gently on the top of her head, moved around the small table and sat down opposite her and smiled.

He threaded his hands between the array of condiments and glasses on the table and Eira did the same until their hands met. This was it. This was what he had dreamed of ever since he had helped her through that awful night when Sion wasn't well. James believed tonight he was the luckiest man alive and every other male guest in the restaurant agreed.

18

Their journey back to London was uneventful and followed a full Welsh breakfast so a stop for food was unnecessary. What Eira found fascinating was the hands free telephone. Every day was a working day for James and phone calls from work on the journey were constant. Eira kept looking around inside the car to try to find the owner of every new voice. Three hours later he pulled onto his drive in Marlow and woke his sleepy passenger. James asked if she would mind waiting in the car for a few moments while he spoke to his sister.

James had intrigued his sister Lucy by suggesting he had a proposition she may like to consider and would she be there when he arrived at his new home. Lucy was definitely the black sheep of the family. Five years younger and similar in temperament to James, she was fiercely independent. She had his swarthy good looks and the privilege of the upbringing of a society woman.

As comfortable with royalty as she was working in a Red Cross charity shop, Lucy had left Oxford University with a first class honours degree in

Commercial Law and promptly declared she never wanted to see another 'bundle' or the inside of a court room as long as she lived. Instead, as a stop-gap she had taken a job as a travel agent. However, this was a role where she erred more on the side of the perk of free travel than the real job of agent. Her patient employers had eventually allowed her to, 'leave and pursue a career which more closely matched her skill set'. She found it difficult to find another job in the short term and was about to default on the rent on her flat when, as often happens in life, her troubles turned into a crisis when her partner and 50% of the rent walked out.

She had never come to James for money and never would, but what she had done was to come to him to complain about life over a bottle of his single malt. As brother and sister they had been very close but had drifted apart over the last few years when James had settled down with his ex-partner. There had been an icy atmosphere whenever the two of them met. James described it like being in a pit with two fighting cocks complete with spurs, walking around each other preparing to strike when either came within clawing range. He decided Lucy and his partner would never choose curtains together so engineered to keep them apart and saw Lucy on her own for lunches in the City.

He was delighted when she got back in touch, Lucy was James's only confidant but even she had not been privy to events that had happened at the stone circle; that was not till now. Lucy's crisis had occurred just before his last trip to Wales so he'd decided to allow her to stay at his new home until she found something for herself.

He hugged Lucy at the front door but he couldn't get her full attention because she was nosily stretching to look over his shoulder to see who was in the passenger seat. He ushered her into the kitchen, sat her down and said bluntly,

"I need a favour."

"Go on."

"I need somebody I completely trust to teach someone, who I love more than anything else in the world, to become comfortable in my world. Will you do it for me please?"

The phrase, 'who I love more than anything in the world,' clinched the agreement for Lucy. These were not words that she had ever heard from him, nor had he ever asked her for a favour before. As James went out to the car to bring Eira in to introduce her, Lucy imagined all sorts of intriguing scenarios; a young child from a developing country, an illegitimate son or daughter from a previous attachment, a pregnant Eastern European woman who has no English? Nothing could have prepared her for the story that was to unfold over the rest of the evening.

Lucy fell for Eira as soon as she saw her and Eira relaxed for the first time in someone else's company other than James's. They fell into easy conversation, James steering it to avoid any questions about the immediate past. There seemed to be a rapport between the two women. They ordered a Chinese take-away much to Eira's delight and together they settled in to the unconventional meal complete with chopsticks and much laughter.

Eira tactfully retired to bed early to allow James and Lucy to catch up. As with all their catch up meals, wine was involved but both remained remarkably sharp. James asked her not to say anything until he had finished his story. She agreed, intrigued, not knowing what a bizarre tale was about to unfold.

He told her the story leaving nothing out, sardonically finishing with, "So that's all there is to it really."

"I need something stronger," was all Lucy was able to say and reached for the single malt. She poured two large glasses, passed one to him and tried to unscramble the last half an hour.

"If anyone else had told me this tale I would have suggested therapy," she said matter of factly, "but because you are the most grounded guy I know who doesn't do fairy stories I'm really trying to understand and believe. Just let me take myself through it all again please, 'cos I'm a bit of a pedestrian thinker. Just so I have this right," asked the incredulous Lucy.

"A year ago, on your birthday, which happens to be Midsummer's Day, you fell asleep on a big rock in Wales and woke up three thousand years ago, right?"

"Right"

"But hundreds of people must fall asleep on rocks in Wales, James. It's covered in rocks. They don't all end up in the Late Bronze age."

"No, I'm sure they don't. All I can assume is that none of them have fallen asleep on my particular stone, in my particular stone circle, on Midsummer's Day. I don't know the explanation, I really don't."

"This is real spooky stuff James. How long ago did all this happen?"

"It all started a year ago, give or take a few days."

"How long have you known Eira?"

"Either a year to the day or half an hour, it depends on which way you look at it. I honestly don't know. I spent a year living with her in her village but when I returned, time had only moved on half an hour."

There was a pause while she swirled the honey coloured liquid around the glass and her mind moved on to other parts of the story.

"And you ended up killing how many Hunff... Huml...?"

"Hunllef. About six or seven, I'm not sure. It was all pretty gruesome."

"Don't you feel any remorse?"

"None at all, don't forget what I did for a living before all this happened. It was surreal; they were just killers, no feelings, no heart, no compunction, animals. They were killing lovely old people. Someone had to stop them and I was there."

There was a long pause while Lucy hunted for more questions. There were hundreds but none she could think of just now. After another long pause she turned to him in a brother/sister way and said,

"James she's beautiful, but you can't keep her. I'm sorry I didn't mean it like that. What I mean is she belongs to a different world, a different culture, it just wouldn't be fair. Of course I'll help you, you knew that before you asked me. I'd do it and enjoy doing it but what's going to happen next Midsummers Day?"

"We go back together to the stone circle and travel back in time three thousand years. When we are back in her time she can choose her world or mine. Whichever she chooses I'll stay with her and her son, Sion. I'll never leave her again," James winced at his crassness. This was his younger sister who he was talking of leaving forever. Apologetically, he said: "I'm sorry I just can't live without her. Lucy, she's my whole world now."

Lucy understood, swirled the liquid around and downed it in one go.

"O.k., I'll give it a trial for a couple of months to see how it goes. If it's not working from Eira's perspective or mine then we stop, deal?"

James came across to her, gave her a hug, kissed her goodnight, put away the single malt, took Meg around the garden, automatically looked up for Barnaby's shooting star and locked up for the night.

The best result ever.

19

Lucy and Eira became close. They shopped together, they ate together, they met friends and slowly as she became more confident it was Eira who was doing the ordering in restaurants and cafes and suggesting places she would like to visit. Lucy's language changed from, 'I'll bring Eira to meet you at the station,' to, 'we'll meet you at the station,' It changed from, 'today I'm going to take Eira to see the Tower of London,' to, 'today we're going sight seeing.'

James was thrilled with the changes and delighted in having two beautiful women everywhere he went, one on each arm. When they went for lunch there were three of them, when they went to the theatre there were three of them. But when Lucy believed James and Eira needed time together she engineered a meeting or an appointment and absented herself. Lucy saw James and Eira growing closer and closer as the days rolled on in their 12-month window. She could see herself suddenly losing, not only her only brother, but also someone who had become a real friend. The possibility made her sad to think of life without them so she concentrated on now.

Eira was an avid learner and soaked up etiquette, fashion and conversation because of her attentive tutor. There were the odd moments where misunderstandings occurred but Lucy, who always saw the funny side of things, brushed these off. In the main, Eira's tuition went according to plan. Eira was the centre of attention wherever they went; she brushed off the advances of potential suitors explaining to Lucy they wouldn't stand a chance against the 'Hunllef'. But with every encounter she became worldlier.

After about eight months of the happiest time of his life James received a wedding invitation. An old friend and confirmed wealthy, titled, bachelor, who James had grown up with in school, decided married life was for him all of a sudden and set a date. The invitation read 'James and Partner (if anyone is lucky enough to have caught you yet) are invited to etc...' James decided he and Eira would go. She was ready.

They arrived at the church, James in morning dress and Eira in a cream outfit topped off with a fascinator, all chosen by Lucy. She looked absolutely stunning. They entered the church early as the organ music was quietly playing and were shown to the right hand side of the church by an usher in a suit that looked as if it belonged to his father. The usher's father was also a larger man than his son and despite the crumpled usher's protestations they sat at the far end of a row. James explained the coming ceremony to Eira step by step.

As the Groom entered the church with the Best Man they spotted James and immediately came over. They shook James's hand but both were looking at Eira. The Groom kissed her hand as only a titled man would and the Best Man all but dribbled. James announced he was delighted to have been invited to the wedding, 'that was never to be,' and they laughed at the oaths they had sworn never to wed, always made under the influence of drink. They agreed to have a beer together and catch up later at the reception.

The wedding march announced the bride and like all women Eira strained to catch a glimpse. The Bride walked alone down the isle and stopped just before the smiling Groom. The ceremony was uneventful, the organ-playing dire and the singing tepid. Long since had James stopped expecting something spectacular or even good from a wedding, they had all been so similar.

The ceremony concluded and the smiling couple walked back up the isle to the hymn, 'Through the Night of Doubt and Sorrow' the Groom's little joke. Then James saw her, his ex-partner. She was sitting two rows from the front as a guest of the Bride. James's plans crumbled. Gone was the idea of a gentle introduction of Eira to just some of his safe friends in a risk-free environment. James's ex was anything but safe or a risk-free environment. Eira was not ready for a meeting with his ex-partner. In fact, neither was he, she was still quibbling about the last bits of the pre-nups.

He decided they would exit the church from the side door as the wedding party made their way through the church at the end of the ceremony. He would get Eira into the car, return to the Groom, give his apologies and head for home. He would choose another event to introduce Eira to his world. James slid along the seat and as unobtrusively as possible tried the side door; the door was locked, James's heart sank. That left them no option but to dutifully follow the wedding procession out of the church.

Outside was bright sunshine, a lovely day for a wedding. The guests were gently cajoled by the motley posse of ushers to walk from the church to the old castle that stood nearby for the photos, the endless photos. The atmosphere was wedding, the chatter was wedding and the weather was wedding. Drinks and canapés were provided to ease the wait. James had lost sight of his ex, which made him nervous, but he talked easily with some old friends he hadn't seen for years. Not once did he let go of Eira's hand. He relaxed only when he saw how comfortable she was in company and the fictitious but plausible story of her past, concocted by Lucy and him for situations such as this, held up to a cursory level of scrutiny.

Heading towards them, James spotted his ex stalking from group to group carefully reducing the distance between them. Suddenly she was there, glass in hand.

"I spotted my car in the car park. I hope you've been looking after it darling."

"And equally, I trust you have been looking after my Aston Martin."

"Sorry darling, had to get rid of it. Not suitable for London driving. Swapped it for a smaller car," she knew how it would have smarted on James.

"So this is the new lady in your life James. You were right she is very beautiful."

His ex reached out and introduced herself to Eira.

"I'm his ex and you are?"

"Eira and I'm pleased to meet you."

"Just remind me, how you two met, James didn't tell me?"

Before James could intervene Eira spoke confidently.

"We share a common interest in stone circles and life in the Late Bronze Age."

"Fascinating, darling, fascinating, I can just imaging the pillow talk in your bedroom about stone circles darling," came the sarcastic reply followed by,

"And how long have you two been an item?"

"Where I come from a year can be a life time. We've lived together for a year, so I suppose we've been together for a life time," said Eira.

"James and I lived together for, God knows how many years, and every day felt like a lifetime to me darling," she laughed affectedly.

His ex's comments were designed to belittle James.

"Ah, so it's you who must be three thousand years old then?" sniped James's ex as she looked straight at Eira.

"We're all getting older, every day we're getting older," calmly replied Eira, not phased by the comment.

"Trust me, three thousand years is a lot older darling?" replied the ex.

"Then if it shows that much I must change the anti-aging creams I'm using," and looking her straight in the eye Eira continued,

"and what will you do?" James coughed, his ex coloured and before the spat could continue Eira pointed out the photographer waving to attract James's attention.

"Must go, always nice to see you," said James coldly to his ex and they hurried away James still holding tightly to Eira's hand. On the way over to the photographer he stopped abruptly and kissed her really hard on the lips and said, "You were great, really great. Why ever was I worried with everything you have seen and lived through, what ever was I thinking about? You are a thousand times the woman she will ever be." And he hugged her again.

Eight months passed and there was still no sign of Lucy wanting to opt out of helping Eira to adapt to 2000 AD. James and Eira attended evening medical classes at the local hospital and amazingly for James Lucy attended too, just to be with them. The year was speeding past and the three of them became even closer.

Lucy had introduced Eira to many of her friends to acclimatise her to society life, much of which Eira hated. Lucy, was thrilled to bits to hear how Eira had despatched herself with James's ex and was now happy to leave her to fend for herself for a few minutes at a time as Eira grew more confident by the day.

James's corporate functions were three-line-whip occasions and if there was no wife then it was the obligation of the senior manager to find a temporary one. James was happy to take Eira who enjoyed the company of some of the wives after the first couple of events. However, she was never out of earshot of James.

The whole plan was coming together and even Lucy was as happy as James had seen her for a long time. She had a dream ticket, to shop till she dropped for Eira and to help her choose presents for their return to her family and friends. Eira's wardrobe now had clothes for every occasion. A far cry from her two shift dresses, one for winter and one for summer back in Llandrillo. They explored Selfridges, Liberty's, Harvey Nicks, Harrods and every boutique in London. They shopped for warmth and fashion alike. Lucy couldn't drag Eira out of the children's departments in all of the big stores. She just couldn't help holding up little pairs of trousers and jackets and wellies and socks and shoes hugging them to herself and saying 'they're just too cute'. A phrase stolen from Lucy amongst others that James would have preferred Eira not to adopt in her vocabulary of 2000 A.D. expressions. Some clothes were bought for her friends' children along with warm winter clothes for Nain and Taid and herself.

20

Beth walked forward slowly, step by step, concentrating on keeping the knife-edge of light on her face. As she neared the outer ring of Stonehenge stones the light widened enough to allow her to see down the light. There, through the mist, an ancient pageant came into focus approaching the stones. There was noise from horns, cymbals and drums; there was laughter and chanting from the procession, all coming from a line of maybe a hundred people. The colourful robes of the priests led the procession up the gentle incline towards the stones. Every person in the pageant carried a shepherd's crook and a bundle and the pageant was making its way up the well-trodden avenue towards the stones. A myriad of people from all walks of life seemed to have come to worship life at Stonehenge. There were the obvious wealthy identified by their clothes; there were the priests identified by their robes and there were the common folk dressed in their working garb. Beth watched the amazing spectacle from her exact position between the two rows of stones.

Then it dawned upon her. She had been right all of the time. Here was the secret. The secret was at night. The night was also the time for light but the reposition of the stones had obscured the moonlight. Nobody could ever have seen it. The secret was that there were two special days, not just one. There was the summer solstice and the winter solstice.

As the procession moved around the outer stones and past Beth's place, one priestess left the throng and came over to her beckoning Beth to join them. Beth was being invited to join the ceremony; she could be seen by a people who lived up to five thousand years ago? The priestess was short and a plump with the white robes of her position fitting her snugly. The pointed hood was off and her long, grey hair hung down, tied in braid. Her head was slightly on one side in a curious welcome to the stranger. Both hands were held out to lead Beth to the procession and join the ceremony. She exuded nothing but happiness. Beth made the instant decision that these people weren't about to slaughter her or some poor virgin or a sacred calf. These were gentle people and tonight they were inviting her to join them.

Hesitantly, Beth reached out and touched the hands of the priestess. Her hands were real. Her hands were soft and warm and calm. The smiling priestess gently closed her hands around Beth's, inviting her to follow. These people seemed to glow with happiness. Beth was caught up in the moment and soon found herself swaying in time with the rhythm of the music.

Beth held the hand of the priestess and mingled amongst the procession circling the stones twice and ending in the centre. Over the noise the priestess explained that people came to Stonehenge to pay homage for the bounty of the seasons. They brought gifts for those unable to support themselves; they were not bent on sacrifice or brutality. Every person in the procession carried a gift, which they deposited in the central circle of stones. These gifts were for the poor and the elderly who followed the procession. There were gifts of clothing, food, wine, beads, and bread and so it went on. Beth's guide explained that when the moon was at its highest every person, farmer, hunter, priests included, took or sent a gift to Stonehenge to give to the elderly and/or the poor. The circle had been built to mark both the summer and the winter solstice. It had been constructed to celebrate the movement of the darkest days of shortage to the days of plenty.

The procession followed the same route in full moonlight to redress the difference between those who had plenty and those who had none. Every month smaller processions were held at lesser circles round the area but once a year the imbalance of rich and poor needed to be redressed and everyone came here, as a pilgrimage, to Stonehenge.

Still now, the priestess explained, in the year two thousand AD they came; their ghostly procession still active for three reasons.

One, to introduce those, who in their lives had believed in stone circles. Once a year the procession invited those believers who had passed from one time to another and introduced them to other believers.

181

They came together to celebrate the good concepts the stone circle had been party to across time.

Two, to continue the ritual of supporting the less well off.

And the third and most important reason of all was to bring the gift of love and peace to a world that needed it now more than any other time in the whole history of creation.

Beth felt privileged and humbled to have been allowed to be part of the ceremony.

When all the gifts had been distributed to the less well off the procession made its way back down the avenue leaving Beth to wave to the priestess. Beth was left with such a feeling of calm...

One week later, Professor Brendon Quail slid slowly and painfully into obscurity. One by one his organs had given out leaving him totally dependant on Macmillan nurses. He died, penniless and worse in his view, undefined in the academic world. His single finale to life was to have been a brilliant presentation at 'Conference' exploding the classical theorists of Stonehenge with unchallengeable calculations. More importantly to him were the accolades that accompanied such a presentation. Professor Brendon Quail, Father of the new Stonehenge Theory. However, failed in life, mediocre in his own research and even failed in deceitfulness he was to see no such accolades. He lived just long enough to see the agenda of 'Conference' and died, screwing it up in anger. Professor Brendon Quail read the words on the agenda and they burned his last breath. 'Conference' was to stage, as the guest speaker, a newcomer to the academic world, a Dr Beth Vaughan whose exposition on the Stonehenge origins had been proved beyond doubt. He died a bitter, lonely, old man blinkered by chasing another researcher's glory, shamed and a failed thief.

***

James sat in the audience watching the slightly nervous Beth walk across the stage to give her presentation. His 'people' had secured a place for him on this most auspicious occasion solely by money. Seats were like gold dust and he sat amongst the great and the good of Late Bronze Age history. Beth had no idea he was there, for the last time she had seen him was when he had acted as a decoy for the security guard. She had been so preoccupied with her preparations for her presentation at 'Conference' that, apart from two messages to say thank you to him, she had done nothing but consolidate her findings for the accompanying paper.

Her presentation began with soft music and some unusual filming of Stonehenge through the day, starting with sunrise and finishing with sunset and the night sky. She had set the scene. She then moved on to explain how the circle had been reconstructed to conform to the then current thinking of the summer solstice. Then, by some very clever graphics she started to move some of the stones into their pre-reconstruction original positions. Superimposing the path of the moon on this layout it became clear that Stonehenge was originally built with two agendas, one to follow the moon and one to follow the sun.

'Conference' questions had been carefully orchestrated and she was able to complement her answers with the aid of further graphics. The presentation was a success and the audience acknowledged her research with a standing ovation, unheard of in the realms of late Bronze Age historians.

At the end of her presentation Beth was surrounded by the eminent in the field and James waited until the great hall had cleared completely of people. She was packing up when he posed his question.

"What was it that you really saw on that night?"

Beth strained to focus on the auditorium because of the bright lights and then, when she saw it was James, she came running down the auditorium to where he was sitting. He rose and took her full embrace. He was as pleased to see her and was so pleased the presentation had been so conclusive and well received for her.

"I'm so pleased to see you. I did ring. I left messages lots of times. Why didn't you reply?"

"I decided to wait till after your presentation. You had enough on your mind and I would have just been a distraction"

"Silly, I would have given anything to see you."

"Same question again, was that all you saw on that night?"

Beth looked at him and hesitated. "You know something don't you?"

"Yes I do, I also have a secret. But mine comes from Moel Ty Uchaf, and if you tell me yours, I'll tell you mine. Deal?"

"Deal. Let me get cleared up and we'll go and have a coffee somewhere quiet."

James helped her clear away and they walked out of the dusty halls of learning together into the bright street. A small coffee shop beckoned and they sat together in a quiet corner.

"It is so good to see you," she said turning to him and rubbing his arm affectionately. "I'm so very grateful for your help that night. I'm not sure I would have been able to accomplish all this if it hadn't been for you."

"Nonsense, you would have found a way."

The coffees duly arrived and she started to tell her tale of that misty night when she looked down the thin blade of moonlight. As she walked across the circle towards the source of the light she explained how she became aware of a procession taking place outside the circle. She described the sounds and the atmosphere, the priests and their coloured robes. Beth talked of the priestess who had led her into the procession and the gifts for the poor and the elderly. She talked about the music, the dew on her feet and the smell of flowers in the night and how that was the original reason for the stone circle but the saddest thing of all was she couldn't tell any one except him. 'Conference' needed proof, real, calculations, tables and observations. She said the last words mimicking the sonorous tone of aging historians. Beth then went on to explain that, to this day, the priestess had told her, they still parade around the circle on special moon nights but now it was mainly to bring prayers for peace and love to a world that was so full of hate and war.

James asked, "Could you go back?"

"Yes, I think I could. One day perhaps, but what about you?"

James told her the full story. He believed she ought to know everything, even about killing the Hunllef. She sat in silence mesmerised by his story. When he was finished she sat back and said,

"Beats my little experience, same question though, will you go back?"

"Definitely, and soon."

There was a pause before she asked the inevitable question. "Would you take me with you?"

"No, but I'll do better than that I'll introduce you to Eira. She's still here but we plan to go back for good soon."

There was disappointment in Beth's eyes at the thought of him leaving, that James missed. There was even more disappointment that he was leaving with someone who meant so much to him. But there was the excitement of her meeting someone from the Late Bronze Age. Could this really be true? Could this man really have been there and come back? Was there a way to travel between the two times? She had experienced a taste herself and knew it was possible. The offer of an introduction to Eira was real and soon and too good to miss.

Over the next few weeks Beth met Eira several times and couldn't help but like this kindly person. Beth asked Eira about the politics of her time and the cultures, of the way of life and religions. This was reminiscent of the conversations James had with Barnaby all that time ago, but here was someone who knew the questions to ask. After all the questions Beth was convinced of the authenticity of the whole story. She was also convinced by Eira. Beth had experienced enough at Stonehenge to understand there were secrets to her stones and here there was enough evidence to make her think she was not alone in her beliefs.

The day came when they were to go and Beth asked the inevitable question.

"Will you take me with you, please, please?"

The answer came back as a strong, 'No,' from James. One person he was sure could travel in time, he'd done it. Two people were a risk but he would take the risk. Three people were a risk he was definitely not prepared to take.

Beth said her goodbyes, wished them well and said to James that if ever he did come back please to call her. He promised he would but made her promise faithfully never to tell another living soul about the secret. Beth agreed.

21

It was Lucy who suggested she drive them to Wales on June 21st, take the Range Rover up to Moel Ty Uchaf, unload the equipment close by and return to stay at the hotel, Tyddyn Llan. She would stay for one day in case something went wrong and they came home immediately via the stone circle. If nobody showed up she would then drive the car to London and return to her life there. She actually enjoyed driving the car, which had been especially designed for off-road driving exactly like on the Old Drover's Road. The car virtually drove itself with all of the on-board computers leaving them all free to enjoy the magnificent views. Who wouldn't enjoy driving it, a top of the range car? James had said she could keep it if he didn't return.

Eira and James carried a rucksack each from the car to the circle. Eira's bursting with presents and James's full of practical things like tools and seeds. A holdall bulged with medical equipment and a crossbow was strapped on the outside of each rucksack. With tears streaming down their faces Lucy hugged Eira at the stone circle and asked if she really knew what she was doing. James and Lucy said their goodbyes quietly a little way away from the circle, Lucy telling him she had never seen him so happy and he should follow his dream. James intimated she would be 'looked after' if he didn't return but couldn't thank her enough for what she had done for him with Eira. Still with tears streaming down her cheeks a lonely Lucy then headed back to the car.

Meg ran about the stones until she was whistled, settling down panting with her paw over James's leg. James and Eira squashed down with their back against the familiar big stone facing inwards. They did look comical but by whatever strange powers the stone circle held the three were soon asleep.

They were awoken, three thousand years earlier in the stone circle, by the rain crossing the Berwyn Mountains in wide wavy sheets. The first thing they did was to examine the charred stones of Barnaby's funeral pyre. Everything was as it had been left that sad day when Barnaby had left to join the gods. The scorched stones were here so they were in the right time frame. Despite the rain, Eira was as excited as a child. She was so looking forward to seeing her family again after a year of absence. They loaded up the rucksacks, carried the holdall between them and headed off down the Old Drover's Road towards the village.

About a quarter of a mile from the stone circle James stopped suddenly and made the excited, chattering Eira stop too. He was listening hard. From behind them he had heard someone stumble. The rain was lashing down and noisy but he was sure he had heard something. The visibility was only about 40 yards because of the rain. Then he heard someone stumble again on the slippery track. After the last time, he was taking no chances and hurried Eira into the scrub. 20 yards into the scrub they turned to see a shadowy, hooded figure ambling down the track. They only caught glimpses of the figure between the trees and sheets of rain. To James, it looked like the figure carried a club. The Hunllef? Not again he thought? Had he and Eira been spotted coming down from the stone circle by one of them? If there was one of them then that meant there would be more close by.

On the other hand, after what the Hunllef had suffered last time this could only be a lone Hunllef who hadn't heard the stories about the fire and the thunder unleashed upon warriors who came to Llandrillo. He gestured to Eira to unstrap her crossbow and load it. She was as good a shot as he was after all his tuition; once loaded he signalled for her to keep very low and hidden whilst he circled back towards the track to tackle the Hunllef. This one looked about the same size as Rat-face from the last encounter, hooded and hunched against the rain. Alongside the track, James elbowed forwards, a bolt loaded in his crossbow; two more bolts were held crossways in his mouth, just in case.

James was right on the edge of the track and the dark hooded figure was stumbling along towards him. James took careful aim and once in his sights he shouted for the Hunllef to stop. The hooded Hunllef didn't hear James shout above the rain and wind and carried on slipping and sliding on the uneven muddy track towards him. James stood up in the centre of the track and shouted again. This time the Hunllef heard him and stopped. The Hunllef was swaying from side to side trying to see through the rain. Then the Hunllef pushed the hood back to see more clearly and raised the weapon to be held in both hands. James shouted a second time,

"Turn around and go back. Have you not heard of the stories of fire and thunder that crash down on the warriors who come to violate this place?"

The figure swayed again still trying to focus. Then the figure spoke,

"James, is that you? You frightened me to death."

James walked cautiously towards the figure, "Lucy, what the hell are you doing here?" When he was sure it was her and not the Hunllef he unloaded his crossbow laid it on the track and put his arms around her, "Lucy this wasn't the plan, whatever are you doing here. By this time Eira had heard her voice and come out of the trees to the track.

"Lucy. Why, why?" was all she said.

A sobbing Lucy explained,

"I went back to the car and just sat there. What was I going back to? What? More of my old life? More loneliness? More debt? More of the same? It just wasn't enough any more. What you two were doing was exciting, an adventure, there would be danger, uncertainty, all the things I dream of. Despite the fact it had started to rain like hell and the only wet weather gear I had was this old umbrella in the back of the car I went back to the circle to try to persuade you to let me come with you only to find you had already gone. I cried and I cried. I'd just lost the two people I loved the most in the entire world in one go.

Then in a mad moment I slid down against the stone you had been sitting in front of just to be close to where you had just been and cried. I know it was silly but just did. I must have drifted off despite the rain. Before I could even consider changing my mind, this terrible downpour in a different place was soaking me. The umbrella was a complete waste of time and I nearly threw it away in temper. I looked about and everything had changed. The circle was different, the car had gone and there were trees everywhere. I had no idea which way to go. All I could remember was you saying that you went downhill to the village on a track. So, here I am. Please don't be cross with me you're the two dearest people in the world and I was never going to see you again, I love you both."

They all hugged and Eira said,

"Of course you can come, but there are no manicure or pedicure parlours where we're going. There are no sushi bars or MacDonald's, email doesn't exist neither do Range Rovers or white-wine-o'clock and you can't get a signal so you'll never be able to order a pizza." Lucy laughed through her tears and James's heart melted; he was secretly pleased she had come.

The three of them, all smiling despite the rain, redistributed the bags and headed off down to the village.

Lucy was in such a good mood. She babbled on declaring that everybody should have a stone circle or a place where dreams become a reality. A forest or a cliff top or an old church, it didn't matter where as long as it was their place, their special place; a place where they could travel in time; an exciting place full of adventure. A place where they could be whoever they wanted to be. A special place where they could do whatever they wanted to do and could be with whoever they wanted to be with.

Eira smiled, the roles were now reversed, she would now become Lucy's tutor.

James was still on the lookout for smoke or other signs of the Hunllef but there were none. At the bottom of the hill where the track levelled out and the forest became rich fertile fields they saw the first house accompanied by the distinct smell of wood burning in the hearth. He decided to call in to see the old woman whose husband had been killed by the Hunllef last time he was here. He banged on the door and called through the rain. An elderly man opened the door, peered out, recognised Eira in a moment and ushered them all in from the rain. There were hugs and kisses from the old woman for James for what he had done the last time. She then introduced them all to the old man who had opened the door.

It transpired that he had lost his wife to a fever 10 months ago and the old woman had invited him to live with her now that her husband was dead. Their chances of survival were increased immeasurably now they were together.

Eira asked if anyone was using his house in the centre of the village for Lucy would shortly be looking for a home. Eira was told that if she wanted it for her friend then she could have it and welcome for what James had done for the old woman.

"There," declared Eira, "not five minutes in my village Lucy and you already have a fine roof over your head."

Lucy thanked the old man with a hug and the three of them left.

Back out into the rain and they ran as fast as they could to Eira's house and burst in. They frightened the life out of poor Sion who believed the Hunllef had returned. He wouldn't let go of either of James or his mother and wanted to know all about her dreams up at the stone circle. In came Nain and Taid from their adjoining house equally excited. Eira held them tightly telling them she had missed them so.

Eira introduced Lucy to Nain, Taid and Sion and then handed Nain and Taid their presents. For Nain, Eira had bought a shawl of the softest, warmest wool, a fleece hoodie and a pair of high fur slippers because she was always complaining about her feet being cold. Lots of laughter and hugs followed. For Taid she had bought a pair of waterproof boots for looking after the livestock in the winter, a tartan waterproof hat with a feather sticking out of it and a large hunting knife. He was over the moon and walked around the house wearing the boots and the hat all evening.

Then she turned her attention to Sion and presented him with his own crossbow and bolts. He was so thrilled and looked to James who immediately agreed to teach him how to use it safely and hunt. In his boyish way Sion announced to everyone in the room they would soon all eat meat every day and they all laughed. James loved every moment of it, the entire homecoming, all the love and the laughter. He sat back and felt so at home with this lovely happy family all of whom were asking questions at the same time. This was a happy place even more complete now his little sister was here, he kept giving her a hug saying,

"You always were unpredictable," and she smiled up at her big brother and understood so clearly why he wanted to be here. When they were growing up there had never been much laughter in their house with their mother and father. They had both felt loved in a formal sort of way, whereas here everything was so real, so genuine, so honest and caring.

While there was a lull, James showed Sion the features of his new crossbow and Lucy looked about the tiny roundhouse. Eira had excused herself and disappeared into Nain and Taid's house. She came back and called to James to close his eyes for his present.

"My present? But, I'm the one who's been away," he protested. He didn't know what was going on but laughingly entered into the party spirit all the same. He dutifully sat down, covered his eyes and waited. An intrigued Lucy watched from the other side of the room alongside Sion, Nain and Taid who were all smiling knowingly.

"You can open them now," Eira said softly and stood there holding the hand of the most handsome little fair haired, blue eyed boy he had ever seen. The little boy could just about walk and stumbled across the room with one hand in the air for balance, Eira steadied him by holding his other hand. Eira then said,

"Daddy, this is Sky."

Until that moment here was a lovely little boy who Nain and Taid had probably been looking after amongst so many others from the village while their parents were working. But an understanding struck James at the word 'Daddy' and he took in a sharp breath and his eyes opened wide.

"James, say hello to your son, Sky," Eira continued watching his reaction.

James lent forward in the chair and was unaware of anybody else in the room. There was just him and his son. He dropped onto one knee to be at Sky's level and caught him just before he tumbled. Sky giggled, righted himself and held onto James's knee for support. The little boy looked up at him with huge blue, smiling eyes. James looked from Eira to Sky and back to Eira trying to comprehend and speak but nothing came out.

"My son?" James's voice eventually trembled for confirmation.

"Yes James, this is your son, Sky."

James held Sky as close as he could and his eyes filled with tears. He was choked with emotion. He couldn't speak.

Then Eira spoke again,

"And my name daddy, is Mair," and Eira presented him with an even more beautiful smiling little girl with long fair hair, the image of her mother.

Eira passed Mair's hand to James. He held Sky in one arm and let Mair's tiny hand wrap itself around his thumb. He swept her up in his free arm and held her close to his chest. The tears were now streaming down James's face. He just held the two little ones and cried and cried out loud kissing each head in turn. He looked up at Eira in wonderful disbelief and then to Nain and Taid and through his sobs he said,

"And you've been looking after them till we came back." They both smiled and gave each other a little cuddle of embarrassment having been in on the wonderful secret.

Sion sensed the twins were becoming a little agitated and nudged Lucy to take Mair and he took Sky off to play outside allowing James to get off his knees and go to Eira and be in one of those precious, private moments, couples have.

"But you never said, in all that time, you never said a thing," James mumbled through his tears of anguish and pleasure.

"I had to be sure you were coming back here to be with me for all the right reasons. And you did. You came back for me alone, not through duty of the children. You have no idea how I have missed Sky and Mair to be with you James, for this last year," and this time the tears were streaming down her face.

Calmness came over them, slowly the two of them realised they were alone in their own little house with their three children, Lucy and grandparents close by, exactly where they wanted to be in a world, three thousand years from this morning.

22

Lucy displayed her toenails to the women folk of the village for the hundredth time. There were squeals of laughter as she took off her socks to reveal the crimson red nails, slightly chipped now but still hilarious to the women folk. In turn they touched them and joked about scratching their menfolk in bed with their rough shapeless nails and ending up with theirs painted in the blood of their husbands.   They marvelled at her dyed blonde hair as it started to grow out and expose the roots, which were a mousy brown colour. Her shaved underarms and legs were also a topic of conversation until Lucy's hair started to grow just like all the rest of the women.

The women folk were fascinated by her underclothes and forever wanted to touch the under-wiring of her bra and feel the lace of the straps.

Lucy capitalised on the attention and in a very short space of time become friendly with all of the women folk of the village. She used these differences to get close to them and when she felt accepted started to teach them a little about feminine hygiene and how to avoid the spread of disease and infections by simple precautions. Washing in hot water was an anathema to the women but Lucy persevered and before long she found everyone was making an attempt. It was when she saw the men folk beginning to wash their hands before eating she knew she was making progress.

Lucy understood quickly that despite the outward appearance of a patriarchal culture there was actually a more powerful invisible matriarchal culture that she could manipulate to the benefit of the village folk.

She taught the women about contraception and how there were some more fertile days in the month than others, how to become pregnant and how to avoid becoming pregnant until their bodies had fully recovered after childbirth. Lucy never felt she was interfering, more she was passing on survival capability to people whose lives were tough enough. She always cleared what she was going to say with Eira to ensure she never inadvertently stepped over cultural boundaries.

Her little house was such a transformation from her untidy student style flat. It was complete when she moved in. Complete with two sets of wooden cutlery and two sets of wooden bowls, all she could want. Although a widower had lived in the house, he had kept it in the traditions of his late marriage, clean and neat. Lucy cleaned her new house regularly and there were fresh flowers on the table whenever James or Eira went in. The twins were always there bringing with them hordes of other children. Lucy loved every minute of the days but the nights she found long and lonely. James and Eira would often find her sitting outside her house looking up at the stars. They would come over and sit with her for a while understanding her loneliness.

One day a line of travellers' carts rumbled into the village. As with any departure from the normal humdrum of Llandrillo's village life, the new arrivals caused consternation. Those in the fields returned to the village and all the children ran behind the parade cheering. The atmosphere was carnival.

That evening everyone gathered around the campfires of the travellers to hear stories of other lands, of legendary folk and their feats. Each story embellished to make it the more fantastic and new colours being added each time it was recounted. James, Eira, Nain, Taid, Sion, Lucy, Sky and Mair all sat together and watched and listened along with all the rest of the village folk. There were jugglers and tumblers, fire-eaters and tricksters, followed by a knife thrower and a dog that did somersaults.

The performance was followed by demonstrations of miracle cure medicines, the real reason for the travellers' presence. A crippled, good-looking, young man hobbled into the arena on rough wooden crutches hardly able to walk and, after one swig of the miracle cure, threw away the crutches and showed the audience he could now run. Other medicines could make men fertile or stronger. The gourds of dreadful smelling liquids were exchanged for food, livestock or corn with the gullible village folk. James and Lucy smiled at the performances. Lucy whispered to Eira she had seen the good-looking young man helping to set up the arena earlier when he carried four of the benches at a time, he certainly was no cripple, in fact she couldn't even see a limp and she had studied him hard. Eira laughed and said, "Limp, he is not!" He was a swarthy young man in his late twenties who had already spotted the unequal mix of adults in James's party.

As the evening drew to a close the children were taken off to bed, some of the adults stayed to listen to more stories and a few of the braver young men stayed to pay for sexual services of the very experienced traveller women. Lucy rose to leave and the 'cripple' came forward and placed a shawl around her shoulders. He offered to see her to her house. Flattered, Lucy agreed. James and Eira smiled.

Lucy and the traveller whose name was Ramos, walked together and he chatted comfortably about where he had been and what he had seen. He described his travels with colour and excitement. He embellished the dangers of a life on the road but talked of waking up every day to a new place, a new opportunity. Lucy listened avidly to this handsome young man. He told her he'd been to the big towns of Caerdydd (Cardiff) and Abertawe (Swansea) on his travels and seen the big sea. He'd crossed rivers and lived off the land with his family all his life. His main enemy were the Hunllef who he'd fought time and time again but preferred to avoid.

For an ex-travel agent who had been all over the world his travels to Cardiff and Swansea seemed little more than local trips to Lucy, but in this time, a thousand years BC, his travels with a train of carts was indeed impressive. She shivered in the night air and he immediately put his arm around her and pulled the shawl protectively over her shoulder. Lucy let him.

As they approached her house he asked if she lived alone? Lucy was taken aback by this forthrightness and her reply of who lived with her included James, Eira and the children. Unconvinced, he asked again, "Do you live alone?" She looked at him. A long time had passed since she had been in the company of such a good-looking man and more importantly, whose company she enjoyed. He had laughed, embarrassed when she enquired about his limp but he assured her, with wicked eyes that he possessed nothing that was limp.

Ramos had the olive complexion of an eastern European and black, shiny, long hair to match. He was slightly taller than her and had the build of someone who had worked physically all his life; his laugh was infectious. To Lucy he smelt like a man, that natural earthy, peppery odour of work and sweat, not as she was used to in the City, men who masked any natural maleness by excessive deodorants and aftershave lotions.

Lucy made him sit with her outside her house and they talked quietly for another hour while she became more comfortable in his company and he patiently wove his ancient verbal magic and web of charm around her. Suddenly, she could resist him no longer; she rose, took his hand and led him inside.

In the morning he was gone. Gone too were all the travellers. Packed up and gone to the next village to wow, to entice then to seduce the villagers into parting with their goods for worthless liquids. Lucy sighed as she looked out from her house and saw the empty space where their encampment had been. Ramos had been an amazing lover, he stood head and shoulders above all her other conquests and he had been so gentle. Not demanding, rough and lacking in finesse as she had secretly expected but kind and soft with her as though they had been lovers for a long time.

Lucy resignedly set about her daily chores sighing regularly about what might have been. The day was long for her and to break the loneliness she asked if she could eat with James and Eira that night. They joked and laughed about her, of all people, being taken in by a 'fly by night' travelling salesman. They finished their last drink of the night and as always, went outside looking for shooting stars to say goodnight to Barnaby. James wrapped his arms around his two most favourite women in the world.

Lucy made her solitary way home in the darkness. She pushed aside the curtain door and was immediately aware someone was there. It was Ramos. He had completed his performance in the next village, cleared up and run the ten miles, travelled through the day with the carts, back to be with her. That was such a romantic thing to do that Lucy felt close to tears. This second night like the first, was a beautiful night. But in the morning, again he was gone. This was like a fairy story, Lucy couldn't wait to wake James and Eira and tell them about her returned 'fly by night' travelling salesman.

The next night Lucy waited and waited. Nothing. She eventually fell asleep with tears in her eyes imagining 'her Ramos' choosing another woman, in another village to seduce with his charm.

It was nearly dawn when her tired body slipped into a deep, deep sleep. In her dreams she imagined the covers being gently lifted off her naked body and a figure slipping silently in bed beside her. In her dream she slid her arm over his body and then they kissed. Softly at first to wake her without frightening her. She opened her eyes wide and this time she really cried, she cried out loud. Ramos held her tightly saying nothing. He was here, he was back. This time she did not sleep after they made love, this time she held on to him not to let him go. This time, if he did go she had decided she would go with him if he would let her. But the morning came and the sun rose and still he was there beside her. They languished in the morning sunshine that tumbled into her house and lit the room. They never let go of each other until mid-day.

Ramos explained he had said goodbye to all of his family the previous night after their performance at yet another village even further away than the last. His mother and father had understood and had always known the day would one day come when he would choose a woman. However, deep down they had always hoped he would settle with another traveller woman. They wished him well but after the initial stoic reaction the realisation that they would probably never see him again dawned and the wailing and crying had begun. After hugs and more tears he had walked the 20 or so miles back to her house. He was here to stay for good. There were happy tears from Lucy and when they finally rose she took him and introduced him to James, Eira and their family.

Six weeks later and again Ramos was gone. He left one night and this time he didn't come back. He'd heard from some other travellers that his family were travelling some 30 miles to the south and the draw was too great. When Lucy heard she rejected the news suggesting to him that it could be any travellers. She made him his favourite food, she made love to him every night and she would do anything to make him stay. But she knew as he looked at the stars one night that the pull of his wandering way of life was stronger than that of any woman; it wasn't personal. She offered to go with him but he laughed saying the life was too hard. And then he was gone!

Lucy received no sympathy from the village folk at his sudden departure, only admiration that she had managed to keep him in one place so long. It transpired that she was the only one who believed she had the remotest chance of Ramos staying in a house for more than a fleeting time. They all saw it as tethering a wild animal.

Eira offered Lucy the profound thought that rather than feel sorry for herself that she had lost him she should cherish the memory of that time she had with him. It was how the village folk coped with the early death of their children.

23

Since their return, James and Eira had fallen quickly back into village life as if they had never been away. They built, with the aid of the other villagers, a purpose-designed roundhouse for treating the sick and injured. They equipped it just as they planned they would in their conversations back in the year two thousand AD. It comprised tables and beds and shelves for medicines and herbs at one end. It had water in barrels and a fire for boiling the water and washing hands. Inside at the other end there was a small clinic area for folk to sit down and talk. Talk about hygiene, cleanliness and dental care.

With some of the village men, James restored the tunnel that had fallen into some disrepair through neglect. As with all threats, the longer it was since the last altercation with the Hunllef the dimmer the pain of the memory.

Engaging the assistance of the village folk was no mean feat. Their days were totally taken up with survival. Not immediate survival but planned survival for the future. Preparation for the winter, preparation for the rains, preparation for every unforeseen circumstance. They tended their meagre crops from morning to night; they tended their stock choosing strong mates from other villages to develop the best herds of cattle. They reinforced their stockades. They fished, they hunted, they ground seeds for bread and in the nights they made love to ensure their survival by propagations. There was little time or energy for other things.

With Lucy's help Eira started a small school. The children, so used to going to Taid and Nain's house, now started to come to the little school which was Barnaby's house converted. There they learned to count, how to sing and how to trade so they would be ready to trade with the travellers without being duped.

James was forever being called out at night to tend to a sick child or the elderly with breathing difficulties. Eira never complained and he never complained. This was what he had planned to do from the very first time he had spent time here. It was when he started to be regularly called to other villages to tend their sick and injured he decided he needed to alter things. Ten miles of walking was OK now and again, but it was happening on such a regular basis that he was never home. This was not what he intended.

Eira started to travel too but James insisted she be accompanied by one of the men from the village on every journey, much to her chagrin.

James gathered the elders together of the surrounding villages around Llandrillo and suggested they select a villager who wanted to learn about medicine and healing and he and Eira would teach them everything they knew. Some of the elders readily agreed but others were wary of the stranger and declined. Five of the surrounding eight villages were represented and in three months James was beginning to make progress. Slowly but surely the frequency of the visits reduced and they were only called out for real emergencies.

When the day's work was done James and Eira's family came together for the evenings. This was the time he loved the best. The children climbed all over him, they laughed and he threw them up in the air and caught them and they squealed with delight calling for him to throw them higher and higher. Sion made things with the children and they played like any family would do in either time. They went for walks together and the children learned about the flowers and the trees. They swam in the river together and they learned about the currents in the river and other dangers.

Occasionally, the children were allowed to accompany them when they went to visit nearby villages and learned their way through the forests. They learned every pathway and what were the dangers of the forest like wild boars and wolves and how to avoid them. Every day they were learning, Sky was the more competitive and adventurous of the twins and was always getting hurt by attempting more and more demanding feats. Mair on the other hand, even at nearly three years of age, was more of a lady, not wishing to demean herself to compete with the boys she avoided their silly games but when she did get cajoled into competing by their irritating persistence she regularly embarrassed them into second place.

The twins grew up with the equivalent of six parents Nain, Taid, Sion, Lucy, and their real parents. There was always somebody doing something interesting and so they were never short of company.

Sion was in the process of building a small stone circle way down in the valley on the other side of the river and Sky would regularly join him. It was on such an occasion that the accident happened. Sion was prising a large stone for the centre of the circle from the quarry face and it was on the tipping point when Sky, who was standing next to him, saw Meg chase a rabbit close to the falling stone. Sky shouted at the dog but Meg was too close to the kill and ignored Sky's calls. To prevent Meg being crushed Sky ran in front of the falling stone grabbed Meg and threw her out of the path of the falling stone. Sky would have been OK too, but he stumbled. The stone continued to fall. A ton of stone fell on Sky trapping his right leg. Sion could only watch as the whole thing happened in slow motion. His mouth was open in a shout but nothing came out.

When the dust from the falling stone had settled, Sion rushed to free Sky only to see his badly crushed leg fast under the stone. Using all his effort there was no way he could move the stone. Desperate, Sion looked for help; there was none. There were no men folk around as the quarry was on a remote part of the Old Drover's Road.

Sion held Sky's head and comforted him while his brain planned at a hundred miles an hour. The little boy drifted in and out of consciousness. Talking to Sky all the time, Sion backed the old horse up to the quarry face and using the ropes he used for securing the stones onto the cart, tied them to the newly released stone that was trapping Sky. Sion then made a short ramp out of timber and stones so that, as the stone moved, it would lift a tiny amount each time off Sky's leg. Oh, how he wished James was there. All of the time Sion was imagining what he would have done had he been there.

The process of building anything near Sky's leg was an intricate one and Sion felt he would only have one shot at moving the stone. All the time he was working, Sion was talking reassuringly to Sky who, with a set expression, understood Sion was doing everything he could. Pain in the form of perspiration ran down the little boy's face.

When the ramp was eventually built and Sion was sure it wouldn't move when the old horse took the strain, Sion went to the old horse's head and spoke softly to him.

From Sion's tone the old horse understood the seriousness of the situation and inch-by-inch took the slack up on the ropes. The stone was big; it was to be one of the centre stones. The old horse leaned into the harness. Gently at first moving one hoof at a time, he moved a couple of inches forward. The creaking of the harness unnerved Sion who wondered if the ropes would take the weight of sliding the stone up the shallow ramp. Then the stone moved, a half an inch at first then another. The old horse understood the task from the intonation of Sion's anxious voice. He moved with great precision. Sion stayed at Sky's side, watching without breathing, watching the ropes, encouraging the old horse with clicks of his tongue. The ramp held fast, the stone slid up the ramp another inch. Sky's face contorted with every movement. Slowly the stone had moved up the makeshift ramp about a foot. Now it was high enough for Sion to get his fingers under Sky's leg and scuft out some of the small stones from underneath. When he was sure there was room to get Sky's leg out Sion pulled Sky free despite the scream of pain.

Sky's leg was badly broken, probably in several places thought Sion. He made him as comfortable as possible and went to prepare the cart.

Sion backed the old horse and unhitched the ropes that were connected to the stone. The huge stone immediately slid back to its original place. Sion then re-harnessed the cart, lifted Sky on board and clicked the old horse to move on carefully. Back in the village he went straight to the little hospital calling all the way for James.

James and Eira worked all day and night manipulating the broken leg back into its original shape. To do this they had to put Sky to sleep several times and build wooden splints to fit his smashed leg. By the morning there was nothing else they could do so James reluctantly went to bed and Eira, Nain and Lucy stayed watching Sky. Before he went to bed

James spent time reassuring the anxious Sion he had done all the right things and if he had been there with him he would have done nothing different for Sky up at the quarry.

It was over a month later before Sky was able to put his foot down with the aid of a crutch. It was another month before he was able to discard the crutch and limp slowly around. But his persistence paid off and eventually he moved about more freely. Both James and Eira said it was too soon to discard the crutches, but when their backs were turned Sky was off and was playing with the other children as best he could.

James watched as the leg healed in a slightly deformed way. He criticised and chastised himself for his inadequacies. Sky's future was uppermost in James's mind and a cripple was not the prospect any woman wanted for a husband in this tough world. Farming and hunting was hard enough with all your faculties; being disabled was a sure sign of an early death. James's second concern was that without proper manipulation as he grew up the leg would become so deformed that he would probably end up not being able to walk at all.

There was a solution, but neither James nor Eira wanted to articulate it for several weeks. It was to take Sky back with him to two thousand AD and during the year have his leg straightened, returning with a strong boy able to cope in this Late Bronze Age. Reluctantly, Eira agreed. She knew the future was bleak for Sky without help and had seen some of the amazing results from the hospital where she,

James and Lucy had been for their First aid courses. There really was no choice.

The summer solstice was in four weeks and after discussing the idea with the whole extended family, including Sky, it was decided.

The next four weeks flew by, with James talking to all of the farmers and hunters about what it would be if they could have anything they wanted to make their lives easier. The requests mainly consisted of tools and seeds for good cereal crops that would be more prolific than their meagre harvests.

The goodbyes were said and all the family accompanied James and Sky to Moel Ty Uchaf. When settled, they all left and Sky and James slipped into the year Two Thousand AD.

24

James led the limping Sky over to the Land Rover and drove back down the Old Drover's Road to Llandrillo. Sky was so excited, not frightened like his mother but watching everything new. His eyes were wide as he watched the dials on the dashboard move as the car bounced its way down the bumpy road. Despite being only three, he seemed older beyond his years and absorbed new experiences like a sponge.

In James's time it was only about half an hour since he left with Eira to travel back to the year one thousand BC and as such there were only a dozen messages on his answer phone. James dealt with them as he drove to London. Sky never closed his eyes once. He asked questions about everything, he wanted to know how the cars stopped and what made them go. He wanted to know which tribe everyone was from and where were their houses.

Eventually, they arrived in Marlow and within minutes Sky was in the pool spitting out his first mouthfuls of chlorinated water. James jumped into the cold water with him to freshen up after the long drive. He loved the closeness with Sky and splashed and played introducing him to rubber rings and lilos.

During the last four weeks James and Eira had discussed what could be done to save Sky's leg. It was obvious that although it had been set as right as they could under the circumstances, it would need resetting. James let Sky settle into his house and slowly introduced him to things that were completely alien to him. The process took about six weeks to acclimatise to life in two thousand AD.

However, life was getting faster in the financial circles in which James moved and he felt he wasn't spending enough time with either the job or Sky. He needed someone who he trusted to look after Sky when he couldn't be there. Someone who understood where Sky had come from. Lucy would have been the ideal person but had left with a group of village folk to trade goods in the South and knew nothing of the incident. He considered asking his secretary but knew she would want to help but was more geared up for corporate life than child minding. Advertising through an agency did not appeal.

Beth had kept the small yellow phone charged up just in case, since James had slipped it into her jeans pocket the night of the moonlit procession at Stonehenge. She never passed it without checking it to see if there was a message, just in case. She nearly jumped out of her skin when its shrill tone went off.

"Beth, it's me, James. Can we meet?"

The idea had come to him when he was showering. He trusted her completely and felt Sky would warm to her in times of his absence.

Trembling, Beth answered it. "James, how lovely. What happened? Are you all right? Where's Eira? Is she all right?"

"I'll tell you all about it. Would it be possible for you to come over here tonight please?"

Beth jumped at the invitation not ever having expected to hear from him again.

That evening the doorbell rang and Sky answered it.

"Hi, my name's Beth, is James in?"

"I'm Sky."

Sky led Beth through the house and into the kitchen.

In the kitchen Beth found James cooking. He turned immediately, put down the oven gloves and hugged her. She was so pleased to see him and hugged him back; she didn't want to let go. Although it had only been a couple of weeks, in this very kitchen, that he had refused to allow her to go back with him, much had happened in his other world. She saw the experience had aged him, only slightly but he looked a little older. This observation had also been levelled at him in the office, the comments being coarse and linking his visits to Wales and regularly looking worn out on return - and sheep.

Beth placed a bottle of ice cold Chablis on the counter and sat at the breakfast bar. James returned to cooking after introducing Sky to Beth.

"So what's been happening to you since we left?" asked James.

"James, it was only a couple of weeks ago that you left and my life is not nearly as exciting as yours."

James struggled to remember the time difference of a full year in his Late Bronze Age life and the time difference of just minutes in his current life of here and now.

"There is one exciting thing. I've been offered, if I want to take it that is, a Professorship at my old university. The money's not good but it will keep my name in the frame of historic academia and as it's a new chair I can take it whenever I want."

"That's wonderful news. Do you hear that Sky, you're sitting next to a Professor?"

James opened the wine and toasted Professor Beth, they both laughed.

For the meal Beth sat beside Sky and chatted to him as if they had been friends for a long time. Sky told her all about his mother and James's homecoming and how Taid hadn't taken his new hat off once since Eira gave it to him, summer or winter. He told her

Nain had said he would wear it in bed if she let him. There was that wonderful belief in any child's conversation that everyone knew who you were talking about at three years old, why wouldn't you?

Together the three of them ate and chatted freely. After the meal James put Sky to bed then took Beth into the lounge with the remnants of the wine and told her the story of Sky's accident and how despite all he had said about not coming back, here he was back again. After a pause in the conversation James ventured the question.

"Before you told me about your Professorship I was going to ask you if you have any time on your hands at the moment but with the new job you'll be pretty busy? And if you did have any time, would you help me to look after Sky through his operations? I would pay for your time and you would be able to stay here close to Sky. It will be for nearly a year until June 21st next year."

"The summer solstice?" asked Beth.

"Yes," confirmed James calmly.

Beth thought for a nanosecond and was about to agree when she made her heart stop talking for her and put her brain into gear first. Here was a guy she thought the world of asking her to help him for a year and then he was going to disappear. Here was a guy who could travel in time, the very thing she wanted in the entire world to be able to do. Here was a guy who was as good as married to a beautiful woman who he couldn't wait to get back to. Here was a guy who was so focussed on his child's recovery that the only result for her would be heartache. James had hardly noticed her. When he did have the opportunity to take advantage of her back in the hotel room in Salisbury he had walked away. Here was a guy with whom she already knew it would end in tears.

There were few times in her life when she found herself with a choice and here was one of them. Her coveted Professorship versus a year of frustration being with someone who would, in the end, walk away and only give her heartache. No, she decided it was she who would walk away. She would pursue her Professorship and carve out a career in the tough archaeological world. She had too good a start to let it go. She was sorry but the cost was too great both career wise and emotionally. She would say no.

Determinedly she opened her mouth and said, "Of course I'll do it." He sighed a thank you and got up to give her a hug.

"If," she continued before he reached her, "if you take me with you next time?"

25

James's 'people' did a good job providing papers for Sky. James had everything he needed to be able to take Sky for a consultation without attracting unnecessary questions. Here was a little boy who had been injured whilst out playing and had received the best medical care available in the third world country where he lived with his mother. Now James had brought him to England to see the paediatric specialists. Beth accompanied James and Sky and was introduced everywhere as the Nanny.

Early in the consultation it became apparent that Sky was in need of another operation to straighten his leg. James asked the question 'if he was your son what would you do?' the consultant's reply was immediate. 'If he was my son I would want the operation to take place as soon as possible.' Decision made.

James was flattered by the consultant's comment that whoever had done the first manipulation probably saved Sky's leg from amputation. James said nothing.

After endless X-rays and examinations where Sky was the model patient, the day of the operation arrived. Sky was dressed in a green gown and wheeled into the pre-op area. James never let go of his hand and neither did Beth. Then came the moment of the anaesthetic and Sky started to count one, two, three, f… As Sky began to dream of home and his sister, James turned to the team of consultants and nurses and, in a voice that only Beth recognised had a slight tremble, said, "Look after him please, he's very special." They assured him they would.

Beth and James left the operating theatre and made their aimless way outside to a coffee bar. There they silently sat with an Americano and a Latte watching them cool down. Beth saw a small tear in James's eye and covered his hand with hers. She smiled an, 'everything will be alright' smile and he rallied. They had been told by the consultant the operation could take up to eight hours and to go and do something. The consultant would call when Sky was ready to go to 'Step Down', the ward staffed by Intensive Care Nurses prior to a normal recovery ward.

Eight hours, a lifetime. James and Beth walked out of the coffee bar and into London's morning bustle. They walked to the Embankment and together watched the dirty boats chug slowly up the Thames. The speed of the boats mimicked time. Their speed seemed to control time, slow, unhurried, chugging. The boats would not speed up, not even in sympathy to hurry the clock around waiting for the interminable eight hours to pass. The boats and time just chugged and ticked as they had always done. Another coffee bar, two more coffees. James struggled the worst of the two of them with the waiting and decided time would pass quicker if he returned to work. Beth made her way back to the hospital to be there in case Sky came around early.

Twenty, half-drunk coffees later and the long awaited call came. Sky was out and the operation had been a success. Tears streamed down Beth's face. In such a short time she had become so attached to this brave little boy. Or was she crying on James's behalf knowing what a successful operation meant?

James ran down the corridor to find Beth waiting outside, "Why didn't you go in?" he asked.

"When he wakes the first person he will want to see will be his Father."

James squeezed Beth's shoulder.

"Thank you."

They went in together to see a very small boy in a huge bed with endless tubes sticking into him. A nurse was stroking his head to gently bring him round. They each held his hand. James leaned over and kissed Sky's forehead.

Sky opened his eyes and a very sleepy smile appeared on his face as he saw his father. Then he turned to Beth and smiled another sleepy smile. Then he drifted off to dream of his sister, his mother and Meg.

Over the course of the next few weeks Beth stayed at the hospital with Sky through the night and slept on a small camp bed beside him. James spent the lion's share of the days with Sky when Beth wasn't there. Between them, they never left Sky's side. On discharge from the hospital there was a continuous round of consultants' meetings and physiotherapy sessions. Sky's recovery was steady and positive. He was obedient with the physiotherapist and the determination on his face showed by his gritted teeth and perspiration. There could never have been a more focussed little boy. It made Beth weep to see his painful progress and James ruffled his hair and held back his tears of pride.

At home Beth taught Sky to read, write and become numerate. For a three year old he was quick to learn; for a three year old who was going through such an ordeal he was going through his ability to learn was incredible.

But there was the fun part too. The three of them played in the garden in all weathers and spent as much time in the pool as they could. Weightless in the water, Sky was fish-like. His leg benefited by the play exercise and he could out-swim James under water. They were a strange but happy trio.

Beth lived in her own part of the house but the three of them ate together and when she felt her presence with Sky was out of balance with that of James, she made excuses and gave them space to be together. Her nights were the hardest when, as Sky's guardian she closed her bedroom door and the woman took over, when she climbed out of her jeans and T-shirt and slipped into lace. Nights when she lay in her lonely bed willing James to tap on her door. For any reason, however trivial just to acknowledge she was there.

She never lost sight of her passing role in their life and as the year progressed the anxiety of having to share him with Eira, Sion and Mair loomed. However, she believed her current distant relationship with him would be her apprenticeship, enough to see her through the coming year, painful as it was. She believed herself strong enough to watch him spend every night with his family, as she did now in part. She decided she would be able to lose herself in her research, documenting every aspect of life in the Late Bronze Age. She would investigate every aspect of nutrition, health, sickness, religion, traditions and hierarchy. Writing up her notes would occupy every second of her days and nights.

Ten and a half months passed and Sky's progress was amazing. He could now walk without a crutch and occasionally he would break into a clumsy trot. The consultant was very happy. Each X-ray showed stronger and stronger bones building around the breaks. James asked Beth to introduce Sky to school life and half a day at a village school became his daily routine. There he befriended a young boy who understood Sky couldn't run and play like the other boys, yet was happy to spend all his time with him. The two became inseparable. The boy's mother encouraged the friendship and one day Sky was invited for a sleepover. This would be the first time

Sky would have been out of either Beth or James's reach. Neither was happy about the arrangement.

Their nervousness was compounded when James's Chairman invited James and a partner to dinner to meet some business colleagues on the same evening as the sleepover. However, the sleepover would solve the babysitting problem, as they would be very late home.

James furtively asked if Beth would join him as his partner in the most boring evening of her life to which she replied, "Compared to what she was used to at 'Conference' she was sure his evening would be an exciting adventure."

James broached the subject of dress code and was curtly put in his place with the retort, "This isn't the only pair of jeans I possess. I do have a clean pair for special occasions!" James was nervous. He had never actually seen her in anything but jeans and either a T-shirt or a denim jacket. He paid her sufficiently well for her to go out and buy a dress but wasn't sure she would choose something appropriate.

On the special day, Sky went to school as normal and then after school, clutching his overnight bag, excitedly he went off with his new friend and his friend's mother for the sleepover.

James dressed quickly for the black-tie dinner and sat at his desk wading through his dreaded emails. Beth busied herself in her room getting ready for the evening. The car would collect them at 7.30pm. On the dot Beth made her way down the spiral staircase into the sitting room. James turned to check her dress sense. There was no need. She really was stunning. A full-length dress in red chiffon open at the back crossed over to hold it in place with gold braided straps. Her hair was up and around her neck was a gold necklace, fashioned in the style worn by eastern Mediterranean Princesses.

James stood up from the desk and walked across to her, he held both her hands and said, "You look gorgeous."

"See, I told you I had some clean jeans."

The car beeped outside and the two locked the house and left.

Prior to the dinner, James introduced Beth as a colleague with an interest in archaeology, which was enough to keep the office predators away. The couple were introduced to the main guests of the evening who were a Greek businessman and his wealthy Greek wife. The Greek husband apologised for his wife who, he said, spoke little English. His beautiful, elegant wife nodded gracefully, comfortable in the formal circumstances even without English. Her society upbringing and engaging smile carried her through when she was introduced to James and Beth. James said he was pleased to meet her and Beth asked in fluent Greek if this was her first time in England.

James's Chairman couldn't be more pleased, the Greek businessman couldn't be more pleased and James couldn't have been more surprised. Beth enjoyed speaking Greek and they sat next to each other all-night and chatted the whole evening through.

James found himself in the quiet times watching Beth. He had agreed to take her back three thousand years in time when he and Sky went back. He had given her his word, and he wouldn't renege on the arrangement. For her part of the bargain, she really had thrown herself into looking after Sky as if he was her own. James could have asked nothing more from anyone.

James listened to Beth across the table. She exuded a comfortable manner and genuine interest in the people she chatted with. She was also very beautiful. How could he have been living with her for the last 10 months and not noticed? Tonight she was absolutely stunning.

The evening was a huge success; the Chairman congratulated James on bringing such a beautiful and talented dinner partner and the Greek businessman thanked Beth for acting as host and interpreter for his wife. James and Beth were invited to the Greek couple's house, an unheard of invitation.

In the car on the way home, after James had rung for the tenth time to see how Sky was, he asked, "And where, may I ask, did you learn to speak Greek?"

"Oh, I did two years in Crete working on a 'dig' called Knossos. Rather than going out on the 'lash' every night I learned to speak Greek."

They unlocked the house and as neither of them had had much to drink James opened some Chablis for Beth and poured himself a large single malt. Beth stood at the French windows and looked out at the garden. In the dark reflection of the windows she saw James behind her just standing looking at her with the two glasses in his hands. The outside lights were still on and showed the garden off in its true splendour in the bright lights and shadows.

James passed her the crystal balloon glass and chinked it with his. They stood side by side looking out at the inviting pool. Suddenly, Beth unlocked the door and pushed open the big double windows, the night was still as she stepped out into the garden followed by James. The two of them walked slowly across the lawn.

Moths danced around the globes of the pool lights and their shadows danced across the marble pool surround. The occasional bat flew silently, following a route flown a thousand times before, wisely watching with all their senses the evening, unfolding below.

An owl hooted a warning to anyone who would listen. The warning fell on deaf ears.

The noise of their steps changed from the silent steps on the dew-covered grass to a slow click on the marble pool surround. Triangular, wet, shoe prints were left by her court shoes on the marble. James's Loakes also left wet prints, close to but not touching Beth's. At the pool edge they stopped, glasses in hand.

"Thank you for everything over the last ten months," said James looking straight across the pool then he turned to face Beth and chinked her glass.

She turned to him and said, "It's been my pleasure. Ten months ago I wasn't sure what to expect, but I can honestly say I've enjoyed every minute."

She relieved James of his whisky glass and said, "Please can we stop being grown-ups now and have a swim?"

She placed the two glasses on a poolside table, turned and unhitched the back of her dress; it fell to the floor in a red circle of chiffon around her ankles. There was nothing else to take off. Beth stepped out of the red circle leaving her wet, court shoes in the middle. She took two steps and dived into the cool water. The splash woke James from his dreamy state and he soon followed suit. From the other end of the pool, Beth watched James dive and she went under water to meet him in the middle. The underwater pool lights lit up the silhouette of her lithe body and he swam towards her. The underwater lights blurred their shimmering forms and they surfaced together in the middle facing each other. Both were wiping hair and water from their faces. James was just able to stand and she steadied herself by holding onto his shoulder.

The water from their movements lapped against the edges of the pool and returned back to them again in waves. Beth put her other hand on his shoulder and faced James. He in turn held her sides and pulled her closer until they touched. Her feet were off the floor of the pool and she swayed to his movements. Then they kissed. He felt her breasts against his chest and pulled her closer. The water returning from the pool sides lapped around this still, single island in the middle of the pool in the early hours of the Buckinghamshire morning.

Beth broke away and slipped under his arms but before she went under the water said, "Race you to the other end." Beneath the surface in the dim lights James watched her graceful movements. Excited by her teasing and feeling it was OK to be a teenager again he caught up with her. Before she reached the other end she felt his hand catch her foot and pull her back. They swam together under the water like otters playing, tumbling and turning until they could hold their breath no longer. Surfacing together they kissed, this time with more passion. She tried to duck under his arms to swim away and tease him again but he held on to her. He felt excited by the contact and revelled in the closeness and the laughter.

Giggling, she wriggled out of his grasp and swam as fast as she could to the other end and flew up and out of the pool in a single movement. James swam slowly watching her movements. Why had he not seen her before? He had seen jeans and a T-shirt but missed the woman. He waited as she collected the drinks and passed his to him. She sat on the pool edge with her

233

legs dangling in the water and he stayed in the water holding on to her leg, his head against her knee.

James watched the droplets of water run down her smooth skin. He looked up and smiled at her. In the strange light her skin looked marble, shiny, newly washed marble. Her legs moved idly circling around and around making swirls in the blue water. Beth was deep in thought. When they had both finished their drinks she took his glass back from him and placed it with hers on a nearby table. She then slipped back into the pool with hardly a ripple.

They made love to an audience of bats and moths and the music of the night creatures. They made love in the water weightlessness. They made love because they were both exhausted by the anxiety of the last ten months, something that started when they left a little boy in a green gown in an operating theatre about to have his leg reconstructed who was now at a sleepover with a friend; a normal little boy. But really they made love because they both wanted to.

The morning came all too soon for both of them. James had left Beth's room some time in the night. They met in the kitchen early. He silently made coffee and Beth silently sipped orange juice.

"Look, about last night," said James embarrassedly, "I never planned for it to be that way. I wanted so much for us to be friends and nothing to get in the way. I've loved your company and nobody could have come anywhere near what you have done for Sky. We shared something special before last night, which I

234

feel I may have now broken. If I have then I'm truly sorry."

Beth listened and after a long pause rose up from her chair and walked over to him. For a long time she looked full into his guilty eyes and said, "Last night was one of the most beautiful nights I have ever had. When we made love it was a demonstration that we shared something special; nothing was broken, something came alive. I've loved being with you both and feel privileged to have shared some of the anguish of the last ten months with you. I understand you can't wait to be back with Eira, Sion and Mair again and I promise never to get in your way. But I will always have had a soft spot for you whether last night had happened or not. I wouldn't swap last night for a sack full of stone circles."

Beth continued, "From my side I'll never mention last night again but I'll think of it often. From your side you must honour your side of the bargain and take me back with you and Sky. As we agreed, I'll only stay for one year and gather as much data as possible. Then I will leave and promise never, ever to reveal your secret. Leaving you will be the hard bit for me, but I've already had a year with you I didn't expect and am about to have another, albeit not exclusively. Please don't regret anything about last night, I don't."

Beth returned to her seat at the breakfast bar and said, "So, are you going to pour the coffee or just keep stirring it?"

26

Beth held one of Sky's hands and James held the other as they walked with their heavy rucksacks up to the stone-circle at Moel Ty Uchaf. Sky was now three and a half years old and tall and straight. He was a normal, happy boy despite his ordeal. He'd been brave through all the frightening experiences of the hospital and operations. Now he held his head high and he walked with just the slightest limp. James couldn't have been more proud of him. However, James was so looking forward to being back with Eira, Mair, Lucy, Taid and Nain. He just couldn't wait. The three of them had gifts for everyone in their rucksacks.

They slowly climbed the last of the hill up to the circle and Beth, who hadn't seen it before, was in awe of its striking position and commanding views.

"I can see why you think it's the best circle," she said walking around the stones, " it's just amazing."

"I have seen it at sunset as the book suggests, but not in this time, it is, just as they say, amazing," said James, knowing now he never would see it in this time again for this was to be his final journey through the curtain of time. His future lay with his family three thousand years ago. He had finally chosen and if it hadn't been for Sky's leg he would never have returned twelve months ago. The trip had been a huge success. Sky's leg was healed, and they were heading back home.

Beth, on the other hand, was filled with apprehension. Although she had met with Eira and talked endlessly about life so long ago it was in the security of James's house, the security of the year two thousand A.D. There was a surreal part to the conversations. As if both James and Eira had visited another country and were trying to explain in the minutest detail what it was like to someone who had never even been out of the UK. This was an historian's dream about to become a unique reality for her. Her safe return alone was her concern; however, her comfort was the fact that James had made the journey several times before.

Puffing, they eventually selected the right stone and settled down, James's back against the stone just as he had done the very first time. Between his legs sat Sky and Beth snuggled down in front of him. The rucksacks were pulled in close. Two minutes of sitting in this position had elapsed and James and Sky were drifting when Beth suddenly got up and said,

"I'm sorry James, I'm not sure I can do this. I'm very frightened." In her heart she had fallen completely in love with James. She'd loved his company over the last year; she loved his compassion for Sky. Despite what she had said the night after they had made love it had had an impact on her. Now she was about to accompany him back to his wife and family and watch him slip away from her forever. She wasn't sure she could do it. This thinking on the other hand was tempered by her age-old dream of being able to return in time to live amongst Bronze Age people. She would learn so much. She was so confused her feelings were in turmoil. She stood there looking at him and Sky leaning back against the stone. The whole situation was bizarre.

James struggled to get up and went across to her.

"Whatever you want to do you must do. I won't try to persuade you either way but I won't come back to this time again."

She looked into his eyes and knew she would have to be close to him for as long as she could whatever the arrangement. She held his hand and they returned to sit at the stone. He smiled and reached over Sky to give her a little squeeze and said reassuringly,

"It will be alright, I promise you."

And they all drifted off.

James came to first. He looked about at the burnt stones from Barnaby's funeral pyre and when he was sure he was in the right place he woke Beth and Sky. Beth woke first and looked about. She blinked and rubbed her eyes. It was the same circle but it was different. The stones were higher than when she went to sleep, the mountains were the same mountains but they were covered in trees. Exactly the same experience James had on his first trip.

Sky woke and asked where mummy was only to be told she was in the village and Nain and Taid would be waiting with mummy and Sion and Lucy. They'd all have a big party when they arrived.

Down the Old Drover's Road they made their way with Sky sitting on the rucksack on top of James's shoulders. Beth walked beside asking as many questions as Sky. They crossed the small stream that led across the road and walked down the last steep bit. They were a happy trio. James and Beth both sang Sky's favourite song as he bounced down the winding road high up on James's rucksack.

As they turned the corner James stopped abruptly. There was smoke coming from the village, a great deal of smoke. James hurried them into the tree line and made them stay well away from the path. When satisfied they were safely hidden James slipped back close to the path to try to see what was happening in the village. When he was close enough to see the first house; the one with the old woman who was now living with the old man from the village, he saw them slumped together in the corner of their yard, her lying over him in a grotesque embrace. Their thatch was smoking, half burnt away as were several others in the village. James slipped back to Beth and Sky's hiding place. Without looking at Beth James said to Sky,

"Take Beth up to Sedd Y Cawr, see if you can find Mair. When you have found her stay in the cave until I come for you all. Look after Beth for me, OK?"

Sky nodded at him, no longer in the safe world of two thousand AD but harshly thrown back into his real world. Sky, the one in charge now at three and a half years of age, took Beth's hand and without looking back started up the mountain.

But Beth stopped him and turned to James, "It's the Hunllef isn't it, they're back aren't they?"

"I can only assume the Hunllef had become desperate to ever come here again. They must have run out of food or the elders who came last time must have died of some plague and these are some of the youngsters. Those who came last time would never venture back here."

He rummaged in the rucksack and pulled out a hunting knife and slipped it into his belt. He regretted he neither had fireworks nor crossbow. He hugged Sky and then turned to Beth. Look after him for me. She nodded and hugged James tightly not wanting to let go.

"Be careful, please, please James be careful."

Beth and Sky made their way up through the trees and soon were out of sight, Sky leading the way. James retraced his steps towards the village.

He slipped silently into the house of the old couple. It had been completely ransacked. The livestock had been taken and the old couple had both been clubbed to death. James shook his head in disbelief. These were all the signs of the Hunllef, perhaps another tribe, perhaps from the west or even from across the sea. They were wandering people. James didn't believe the first tribe would ever have returned unless they were absolutely desperate. After the carnage he had created on them last time, nobody would want to come back and tackle him again.

The village was eerily quiet. A feeling of foreboding was welling up in James's stomach. His experience of the Hunllef filled him with dread. Nothing could prepare anyone for their brutality. Their disregard for human life sickened him. His family was here. His future was here; this was the life he had chosen. Smoke curled up from the thatches that were still smouldering. Some thatched roofs were partially burnt off exposing charred rafters like blackened ribs of a beast where half the yellow fur had been burnt off the carcass.

James's first concern was for the village children. The most vulnerable, the tiny ones, the children who would be taken as slaves to these horrible, horrible people, these animals. Their life would be one of an incomprehensible hell. They would be worked till they fell over and when of no more use then dispatched with no more compassion than killing a rat. The girls and young women would be used for breeding. James headed straight to the tunnel exit in the trees. If the children had escaped through the tunnel then there was a chance they would get to Seth y Cawr, where he had just sent Beth and Sky. If they hadn't God alone knew where they might be now.

James stopped short on his way to the tunnel exit having to pick his way through dead Hunllef. Each of them had been shot through the chest or head and their horrific wounds bore testament to the power of the crossbow. James counted 14 dead. There must have been one hell of a battle. Each of the Hunllef seemed to be heading towards the exit of the tunnel. James stepped in and out of the dead and eventually came to the tunnel exit. There to his horror he found Lucy, crossbow still loaded ready to fire. She had been hit with a single fatal blow to the back of her head. She was cold. Just behind her he found Sion, crossbow at his side but Sion had a Hunllef arrow through his chest. James could only imagine the scene.

The Hunllef must have come at night with no warning. Sion and Lucy would have taken the crossbows up to the exit of the tunnel to make sure the children got away safely. As the Hunllef realised the children were escaping and not knowing how, they would have scoured the village and beaten everyone to death till someone told them where the exit was. Then they would have rushed there and been met by a barrage of crossbow bolts.

Sion and Lucy would have been terrified by the onslaught but hopefully, held them off till all the children were safe. Then James saw another Hunllef sitting against a tree, only feet away from Sion. In his stomach, up to the hilt was Sion's hunting knife.

Either Lucy or Sion must have killed him. The tears ran down James's face as he hugged his cold, dead sister Lucy and Sion. He rocked them back and forward in sorrow. Lucy had wanted to come here for adventure, for excitement, for action, to leave her mundane job as a travel agent and enjoy life. She had only lived through two years of her dream and the Hunllef had cut it short.

James had watched Sion grow from a weak, sickly child into a strong young man and his deeds, with Lucy this night, had probably saved the lives of all the village children. This would be the legacy left by Sion, a whole generation of village children saved by his actions. In a strange way James could feel nothing but pride for him. But as Sion lay there, neither could James think of anything other than the complete waste of two beautiful lives. How he hated the Hunllef.

Despite the sickening sights, James's senses were still on high alert and he decided to make his way towards the centre of the village. He collected up the few remaining crossbow bolts and Lucy's loaded bow. He retrieved Sion's hunting knife from the dead Hunllef and pushed it into his belt alongside his own. Crouching down he threaded his careful way between the destroyed houses. It was between two of the houses he came across a dying Hunllef. The Hunllef lay on the ground holding his side, his bloody fingers stuffed into his agonising wound, his face was contorted in pain and his free hand clawed at the dirt to relieve his torment. James recognised the wound as one of a crossbow bolt, ragged and torn. Even

James and his hate of the Hunllef winced at the gaping hole and could only imagine the pain the Hunllef must be in.

However, close by in the dirt, alongside the groaning Hunllef was Taid's tartan hat, the gift from Eira. Imagining what he was about to find at Nain and Taid's house James despatched the Hunllef with an animal fury, killing him for every person in the village who had ever been hurt by these conscienceless marauders. In his terrible fury James stabbed and stabbed at the Hunllef long after he was dead till he couldn't see for his tears. He sobbed and sobbed as he lunged at the inert body. Eventually, he realised the futility and wiped the blood from his hunting knife on the Hunllef's greasy fur tabard and then disgusted, wiped it again in the grass.

James composed himself as best he could and moved steadily between the houses. Having just found a living Hunllef he moved warily, expecting to find others. He had no plan but he had a crossbow and two hunting knives. At every turn there was bloodshed. Villagers were dead everywhere. Killed in the traditional way of the Hunllef by a huge blow to the back of the head. There were friends of his, there were the old and the young lying together. With Lucy's loaded crossbow raised he continued inching his silent way forward making gruesome discovery after gruesome discovery.

Further on he saw the bodies of Nain and Taid sprawled out in their yard. There was blood all over them. James turned and was sick in the corner of the yard. He felt he couldn't stomach any more bloodshed. When he finished retching he rose from his knees and wondered if he might have alerted any lingering Hunllef. Being sick in the corner of a yard with his back to the world was not how he wanted to start his next encounter with one of them. James carefully looked inside their house and saw the entrance to the tunnel exposed, the rug pulled away revealing the escape route.

There was just one more place he had to go to and his heart was desperate to avoid. Was there any chance? Could she have been called to another village to tend the sick? She had missed the last encounter with the Hunllef; she had been up at the stone circle. Could she have gone there again? It was so unlikely. Eira knew Sky and James were coming home today. She would have prepared a homecoming. She would have dressed to meet them. She would be somewhere. Maybe she had gone with the children?

Creeping across Nain and Taid's yard, senses still on high alert, he approached the high wicker fence separating their yard from Eira's. His breathing had stopped, his heart was beating like a drum roll. He tried to look through the closely woven thick fencing but couldn't. He raised his head slowly and looked over. There was Eira an arrow through her chest lying face up on the ground. James stood up not wanting to believe what he was looking at. Her hair was loose and her face not contorted as he expected but calm as if she were asleep.

James pushed the wicker fence aside and moved slowly towards her. Was there the slightest chance? He knelt beside her and touched her face, she was cold. He snapped the Hunllef arrow shaft and cradled her head to his chest. Holding her tightly, he let out a long lasting, guttural cry of "no…" His fraught call of many seconds could be heard all over the village and beyond. He didn't care if there were Hunllef still around or not. He was beyond caring. He had lost the most precious person in the world. Sky and Beth heard the pitiful cry at the same time. Sky looked up at Beth and said, "Daddy," and let go of Beth's hand and started to stumble and slide back down the hill towards the village. Beth caught up with him within 20 yards and held him tightly. She whispered in his ear, "Let's go and find Mair and then, if it's safe, we'll go and find Daddy." Sky was looking down at the village and knew from that awful sound something was terribly wrong.

One by one the villagers who had fled to the forests came back to see the destruction they had escaped, killing any wounded Hunllef and trying to assist the distraught villagers. They came across James still cradling Eira's head. There was nothing to do, nothing to say, they sympathetically put their hands on his shoulders and left him to his grief.

They respectfully collected the village dead and carried them to their burial site. Here they lay them out in their family groups, some groups of two, some of up to six. Nain and Taid they lay beside Sion and Lucy and then went over to Eira's house. James had already wrapped Eira in a white cloth, cleaned her face and combed her hair. He wouldn't let anyone touch her but with tears running down his face carried her, on his own, to the site of her burial. He laid her between Nain and Taid and arranged her so that she was holding both their hands. Sion and Lucy lay one either side holding their other hands.

By this time the children were being brought back to the village from Sedd Y Cawr. As they came down and saw the sight of so many bodies the children's crying and calling for their mothers was heartbreaking. What happened next was testament to the village and its stalwart folk. Those children whose parents had been killed were sympathetically taken by some of the older womenfolk to say their goodbyes and then gently introduced to another family who comforted them through their grief. Not one child was left out, not one orphan was allowed to cry alone. From that moment on, each orphan had a new family and their life would continue, albeit with new parents.

Beth held James as he knelt and sobbed by Eira. She held him as he shook in his grief. She hoped one day she would be able to feel that level of love for someone as she was seeing now between James and Eira.

Sky and Mair had said their tearful goodbyes to their extended family and were quietly being taken to another family that had only one child by a well-meaning elder of the village when James suddenly realised what was happening. He rushed over and thanked the elder and the family for their offer of kindness but lifted Mair in one arm and Sky in the other and, walking back to Beth, said to all the village, "They're staying with me, staying with me for ever," and he kissed each on their heads. All three were crying. The elder of the village and the new family understood.

Beth took over and tried to soothe away some of the children's grief. She held all three of them together in a huddle. Then, decisively, she took Mair's hand in one hand and James's hand in the other and gestured for Sky to take James's other hand and the four of them, side by side, without looking back, started their last walk ever, up the Old Drover's Road and back to the stone circle at Moel Ty Uchaf.

The End